AWAKEN

WOLVES OF TIMBER FALLS

CASSIE LAELYN

This is a work of fiction. Names, characters, places, and incidents are either the product of the author's imagination or are used fictitiously, and any resemblance to actual persons living or dead, business establishments, events, or locales, is entirely coincidental.

AWAKEN

COPYRIGHT © 2022 by Cassie Laelyn

Cover Art by Bookcoverology

Proofreading by More Than Words Copyediting and Proofreading

First Edition 2022

Bloodlust. Deceit. A cure worth killing for.

After hunters attack Timber Falls leaving a trail of destruction, Layla loses hope of ever restoring peace. Until she finds Wyatt Hale—the mysterious yet gravely injured hunter—hiding under her porch. Healing him is a no-brainer. Only, his swoony dimples and sinful whispers blur enemy lines. When Wyatt reveals a traitor in her pack, their forbidden desire becomes even more dangerous.

Now, Layla's torn between her duty and trusting a bloodthirsty killer who's supposed to be her enemy.

But what if those closest to her are the biggest threat?

For you, for renewing my faith in magic

chapter one

Layla

Blood drenched the grass. Dark red blotches, seeping into the earth around my feet. Everywhere I stepped, another layer coated the soles of my boots. Enemy blood. Shifter blood.

The sickly stench of death layered the cool winter air until I could no longer smell the pine needles. Bile rose in my throat as I recalled the lives lost tonight. Not only from our pack. All lives.

Hunters had attacked. Ambushed us. And they left a bloody trail of destruction.

I paused by a fallen tree branch, dragging the toe of my boot through a pile of blood-coated leaves. A dull ache constricted my chest as though invisible hands squeezed my ribs. The pressure so great I didn't know whether to scream or collapse.

We'd grown complacent over the past few months. Too relaxed. And not just Timber Falls. Neighboring packs had resumed gatherings, travel, allowing their pups to venture out alone.

Now, we'd all paid a hefty price for those mistakes.

Exhaustion settled deep in my bones as I surveyed the carnage. Fallen branches, gashes in tree trunks from wolf claws or blades, drag marks in the earth from someone removing an injured shifter. Or a dead one. God, the blood. So much painted the ground that at any moment I imagined the trees sucking it up and changing their leaves to crimson.

I turned away even though I knew I couldn't escape it.

I should head back to town with the others. After the attack, it would be stupid to stay in the woods, especially alone. Safety in numbers had been our motto for years. A hunter wouldn't attack a group of shifters.

How horribly wrong we'd been.

Despite knowing better, I couldn't go into town. I couldn't stomach their looks.

It wasn't your fault.

You tried your best.

There's honor in dying to protect the pack.

No. That was utter crap. Those shifters died because hunters attacked our pack. They died protecting their families.

They died because I couldn't save them.

Besides, Trey had accounted for all the hunters. There weren't any left alive.

I was safe.

Numbness seeped into my limbs as I stared at the dark stains smeared over my palms. So much death. All because of a war started long before I was born, when an ancient coven of witches tried to eradicate shifters by turning themselves into beasts. Bloodthirsty hunters.

Now, descendants suffered the consequences of their ancestors' craving for power, and instead craved something more sinister: shifter blood.

Death. So much senseless death.

Father would never allow this to happen again. This battle was a turning point. He'd declare war against hunters, possibly witches. He wouldn't stand back and accept defeat, not now. Not after a group of hunters planned and orchestrated an ambush on our pack.

There'd never be peace.

Everything I'd worked for died on the blood-soaked ground.

Wiping my palms on the thighs of my jeans, I inhaled a ragged breath. Despite every instinct telling me to return to town with the pack, my feet wouldn't move.

"Layla," a familiar voice rumbled from behind me making me jump.

I turned, facing my father, Alpha of Timber Falls. The one who'd led his pack into battle tonight.

His voice softened as he placed a gentle hand on my shoulder, bending so we were eye level. "I know you don't feel it, but you did everything you could tonight. You saved countless pack lives."

Not enough though.

I nodded, not trusting my voice, or the tears that threatened to never end if I let them fall. Weakness wasn't in my veins, but tonight it floored me.

I peered down at my hands again. Defeat. This was what it felt like.

He wrapped one arm around my shoulder, pulling me against his chest. He smelled familiar, like rugged pine mixed with the comfort of home, but the underlying metallic scent of blood coated my throat. I drew back. I couldn't stand it any longer. If I stayed in this forest, with blood-stained hands for another minute, I'd snap. And if that happened, I feared I'd never recover.

My father kissed the top of my head. "I need to debrief the pack. Let's go clean up."

I stepped to follow but stopped.

I couldn't do it. I couldn't face the pack. Not tonight. Not when all I wanted was to scrub my hands until the skin returned to ivory. Though, I feared it would never be the same. Centuries of war, of bloodthirsty killing, of senseless death would stain my hands forever.

I twisted out of Father's embrace. "Actually, I'd rather...stay at home tonight."

He tilted his head, studying me. One thing I knew about my father, he chose his words carefully, he always had. I figured the trait made him a better alpha. He never took a wrong step. But now, I could tell he took the time to choose words that would empower me rather than make me cry.

His expression softened, his midnight blue eyes deepening even further. "Don't blame yourself for the decisions of others, Layla. Hunters attacked our pack. They killed our shifters. Not you. You saved them."

I shook my head as the anger bubbling in my belly thundered over the grief. The last thing I wanted was to argue with Father, especially tonight, but I had only so much strength left. "No death is warranted. Yes, hunters attacked our pack, but our pack slaughtered them. They didn't just kill them, end them quickly, they *slaughtered* them. Ripped apart their flesh. Those hunters were once witches. Once..."

My throat closed preventing the rest of my sentence. Just as well. I remembered hunters were once basically humans with magic, but that didn't mean my father agreed. Bloodlust was bloodlust in his eyes. No matter who it came from.

I exhaled a slow breath, hoping to soften my father's protective instincts. "I'm exhausted. I just want to decompress." I looked up at him so he could see the truth reflected in my eyes. "I need to be alone. I'll check in with you in the morning."

After a moment of tense silence, where I thought he'd disagree or pull his alpha card and drag my tired ass into town, he nodded. "Keep the door locked. I'll send Trey to check on you."

I refrained from rolling my eyes because that wouldn't help my cause. But seriously? I didn't need protection, especially from Trey. No hunters had escaped tonight's bloodbath.

Instead of debating my independence for the umpteenth time, I simply lifted to my toes and gave Father a peck on the cheek. "Thank you."

"Make sure you call if you need anything and text me when you get home."

"Yes, Father."

Before he changed his mind, or heaven forbid, sent someone to escort me, I turned and followed the path through the forest to my cabin.

Lost in my head, I numbly weaved through the trees, diverting my gaze from every dark stain, focusing only on my destination. The air gradually freshened. Rather than a choking stench, the blood became a faint scent lingering in the background. Probably because it still covered my clothes and hands.

About five years ago, I convinced Father to build me my own place on the wolf reservation. I loved him more than anything, but being his only daughter, his only offspring, meant the urge to protect the pack's future alpha was strong. Overbearingly strong. Not helped by the fact my mother passed while giving birth to me.

My father had years, centuries even before he'd handover leadership, his talk of retirement was a tease. It had better be. I wasn't ready to lead the Timber Falls pack, especially not now.

"Lay, wait up."

I peered over my shoulder and waited for Baker, wearing only a pair of jeans, to catch up. With all the ink down his arms and those ripped abs, I could understand why half the females in the pack swooned over him. Except me, because...eww.

"Please tell me Father didn't send you to escort me home."

He scoffed. "As if I need a reason to make sure my favorite cousin arrives home safely."

This time I did roll my eyes. I was his only cousin.

Baker bumped my shoulder with his, and we fell into step. To be honest, the company was...nice. Baker and his brothers had always treated me like their sister, more than their cousin. But with Baker it was different. He wasn't only closest to me in age, he was also my best friend. And, well, he probably knew me better than I knew myself.

"How's your mom?" I asked, swallowing the sick feeling creeping up my throat.

"She's fine. Cussing at my old man for fussing over her." He shoved his hands in the pockets of his jeans before kicking a random stick. "The wound on her leg is healing already, thanks to your quick thinking."

His mom was one of the lucky ones, but I didn't say it aloud. Even shifter blood had its limitations as we'd all seen tonight. As Father had seen with my mother.

"What's the deal with heading to your place? I figured you'd join the other healers at the infirmary."

I shrugged. "I've done all I can tonight. I just need some time to...process this."

"I get it."

My shoulders sagged with a deep exhale when I spotted my cabin as the tree line thinned. A simple wooden cabin with a front porch and loft. I didn't need much. In the beginning, I came out here on the weekends, but lately, I'd spent more time in town. I hadn't realized how much I missed it. How much I needed it.

Out here, no one depended on me. For a short period of time, I could forget I was a pack healer, Rhett St. Claire's daughter, and next in line for alpha. Out here, I was simply Layla. A twenty-seven-year-old wolf shifter, lover of ancient history, books, and spicy merlot.

At the bottom of the porch steps, I turned to Baker.

"I'm going to head back to town and check on Mom. I'll text you later."

I nodded, so thankful he knew me well enough to give me space. Even though it likely irked every protective bone in his body.

He turned to leave.

"Baker?" When he glanced back at me, I said, "Thanks."

He gave me a curt nod before jogging in the direction of town.

On the porch, I lifted the rustic flowerpot and grabbed the front door key.

Someone coughed.

I froze, fingers curled around the key, crouched beside the flowerpot. Cocking my ear toward the forest, I listened...and listened, until I swore I'd imagined it. Events of tonight played havoc with my imagination and had clearly shot my nerves, making me jump at the slightest rustle.

Straightening, I slid the key into the lock.

The cough came again, this time more of a gurgle as though the person struggled to breathe. Not an animal. A person. And not my imagination.

After battle, shifters usually returned to human form, especially if injured. As though their animal knew the best way to heal was to shift. But my father accounted for all our pack, those alive and...dead.

My heartrate kicked up as the gurgling sounded again.

I couldn't ignore it. Someone was out there, close by, and on the verge of death. I needed to help them. What if it were an injured shifter from a neighboring pack? What if it were a human caught in the bloodshed?

I couldn't just stand here and do nothing. Not ever, and especially not after tonight.

Leaving the key in the lock, I crept down the stairs, scanning the small clearing in front of the cabin. No one. The person coughed again from behind me, this time ending in a sickening wheeze.

I raced around the rear of the cabin, scanning the yard. Still no one.

Where the heck were they?

Something made me spin back to the cabin and crouch to peek under the rear porch. Bingo. A guy, mostly concealed in darkness, lay face down in the dirt.

On my hands and knees, I crawled under the timber porch to assess his condition. Dark short hair, broad shoulders and so many tears in his shirt it clung to his torso by only a few threads. His long, thick legs clothed in torn jeans stretched father under the house. One boot missing.

With only the filtering moonlight, I didn't recognize him, but a few shifters from neighboring packs had helped us tonight. He probably belonged to one of them.

I scanned his body once more, looking for obvious wounds and found deep claw marks in his side, oozing blood.

Why would a wolf attack another shifter?

The guy wheezed again. Blood sputtered from his mouth onto the dirt.

It didn't matter whether I knew him, or which pack he belonged to, I needed to save him. This war had spilled too much blood already. He'd clearly sought safety under the porch while the rest of the pack had finished off the hunters. Once I helped him and he was out of immediate danger, I'd call Father to take him to the infirmary.

Shuffling closer, I tentatively swept thick, dark hair off his forehead to better see his face. "I'm here to help you. You're going to be okay."

His eyes shot open. Bright amber vertical slits narrowed in my direction.

I sucked in a breath, scrambling backward.

This guy wasn't from my pack or any other. He wasn't even a shifter.

He was a hunter.

chapter two

Wyatt

An angel crouched before me, cast in moonlit shadows, with long, platinum hair framing her heavenly face. Her vibrant blue eyes reminded me of glaciers I'd only ever seen in movies. I expected the angel of death to be less...beautiful.

I wasn't ready to leave, not yet. But the plan had failed. Just as it had every time before that.

I'd failed *her*.

Darkness washed over me from all directions. Ominous waves sucking me under, deeper and deeper until pressure squeezed my chest, stealing any remaining air from my lungs. I mentally reached for my magic only to come up empty. I'd gone too far this time, pushed myself beyond the point of no return. The burning in my side faded. So did the agony searing through my veins. In their place, numbness spread through my limbs, flowing from the top of my head all the way down to the tips of my toes.

Not long now.

Soon, I'd enter whatever world lay beyond this one. Soon, the pain, the memories, the failure, would end.

The angel crawled closer, whispering to me, but I couldn't understand her words over the constant buzzing in my skull. Her warm, soft hand touched my cheek, soothing any lingering unease. I fought the darkness, holding my eyelids open for a little longer, mentally capturing her beauty to take with me into the next life.

Her gentle touch swept sticky, damp hair from my forehead. Her lips moved, speaking to me again, but it was useless. I no longer had the energy to listen. Besides, words didn't matter, not where I'd go. Words wouldn't change a thing I'd done up to this point, the lives I'd taken, the destruction I'd caused.

It wouldn't bring Ellie back.

Thick liquid bubbled up my throat. I coughed, trying to clear it, only to inhale a mouth full of dirt. My lungs squeezed, gasping for air.

The angel's eyes widened for a split second before they narrowed. Her chin lifted. Determination. I knew that look. I'd seen it countless times in Ellie before she...

No, I wouldn't think of her now. In these final moments as the angel took me, I'd think of only those rare times of happiness.

Moving closer, the angel's sharp gaze darted left and right before settling once more on me. I was ready for her to take my soul. Long ago, I had accepted my fate even though I fought for a better one, and now I'd pay my penance.

The moment I surrendered, my heavy limbs sank against the earth, and I closed my eyes for the last time, welcoming death.

A slight burn lingered at the back of my throat. It felt like I'd swallowed a shit load of coal which made absolutely no sense. Who would do that?

My muscles wrenched as waves of feverish heat rolled through me. My stomach clenched and unclenched.

Soft, quiet footsteps padded from behind my head, around to my side. I didn't dare move or open my eyes, instead, I let my heightened senses paint a vivid mental picture of where the hell I was.

A thin layer of smoke lingered in the toasty air, most likely from a lit hearth rather than a campfire given I didn't sense I was outside. Gentle heat warmed one side of my bare chest. Clearly, I'd lost my shirt. My senses snatched onto another scent floating in the air. Lush. Feminine. Wildflowers with soft notes of spring. The alluring scent of moonlight, which confused the hell out of me. How did moonlight even smell?

Discreetly, I curled my fingers around the thick, cushioning blanket beneath me.

Someone removed the damp cloth draped over my forehead before replacing it with a cool one. Visions of a silvery-haired angel with piercing blues eyes appeared in my mind. Delicate fingers twisted my arm and pressed against the inside of my wrist. I held deadly still, trying to remember where the hell I was and how I got here.

Hazy fragments drifted through my mind. *Tracking a wolf...a fight...bloodlust...surrendering to the wicked curling in my gut...forgoing a cure...*

Would it ever end?

Those same fingers eased my arm back by my side. Next, she peeled off something sticky taped to my stomach so agonizingly slow, I clenched my teeth, gritting through the burning pain. Had she never heard of the expression to yank it off quickly? When I thought I'd pass out again, she paused before smoothing the edge back down. I tried not to think of her touch, and the strange heaviness it caused in my chest. Pain clearly made me delirious.

As quietly as she'd come, her footsteps padded behind my head once more, fading away. Alone again, I slowly opened my eyes. Blurry silhouettes appeared, and I blinked a few times to clear my vision. Without moving my head, I scanned the room—a vaulted natural timber ceiling, two oversized windows with the drapes drawn tight so no light escaped around the edges. Must be night. A lit hearth to my left, leather reading chair straight ahead, plus the couch I lay on made up the living room. A log cabin of sorts. But whose? Was I still in Timber Falls? If so, I needed to get the hell out of here quick.

I'd hitched a ride with those hunters, but things had backfired.

When I first saw the angel, I swore death had come to take me. It now appeared I was still—

"You're awake."

I startled, having not sensed her behind me. Clearly, I was more injured than I realized. I reached for my magic once more but again came up empty. Not even a spark. I'd never lost touch with it before, and not having access was more dangerous than waking in a stranger's house.

Slender jean-clad legs rounded the couch to crouch by my side. I turned my head to her. Something foreign, deep within my chest tightened as my gaze locked with hers. Vibrant blue eyes, dark platinum hair, thick, long lashes. Heavenly beauty.

My angel.

I opened my mouth to speak but only managed a raspy grunt.

She eased a metal straw between my lips. "Drink."

Christ. Her voice. Maybe I was dead. That would explain why I couldn't use my magic. Or my brain.

The second the cool liquid hit the back of my throat, I coughed, spraying it over her face.

Nope. Drinking water wouldn't burn like acid if I were dead.

She cursed under her breath and wiped her face with the sleeve of her shirt. Once cleaned up, she glared at me. "Drink *slowly*."

Dumbass. She hadn't said it, but the insinuation was loud and clear.

When I nodded, she returned the straw between my lips and watched me, her eyes narrowing as I took a slower sip. The fire soothed in my throat. But before I finished, she removed the straw and set aside the cup.

"Where..." I croaked.

"Where doesn't matter." She removed the cold cloth

from my forehead and placed it beside the cup. "You're only here until you're well enough to leave."

I studied her. Her eyes were gentle, alluring, caring, yet alert. I had a strange feeling she either knew who I was...or what. Inhaling as far as the wound in my stomach would allow, I sifted through the scents to determine if she was a hunter I hadn't seen with the group. Nope. And even though she'd found me deep in wolf territory, she wasn't a shifter either. Had she been, I would've smelled her even in my unconscious state.

Just a regular human. That, I could deal with.

Bracing my forearm on the cushiony couch, I pushed myself into a sitting position. Fire raged through my torso, and I grunted, leaning forward to cradle my stomach. Not that it helped.

The blanket draped over my lower half slipped down until I realized I wore nothing but boxer briefs. She'd... stripped me. As though she'd heard my thoughts, she shoved a pair of jeans in front of my face. "Hopefully, these will fit. Your clothes were blood-soaked."

Standing, she faced away as I pulled the jeans on, which only reignited the searing heat in my side. I left the top button undone because, well, clasping it required too much energy.

"Thanks."

She turned back around and perched on the edge of the coffee table facing me. "The claw marks were deep, causing a lot of internal damage. Add on top of that an infection, and you're going to feel like death for at least a few more days."

I nodded, clamping my teeth until the pain eased a

notch and I could sort of breathe again. "What's your name?"

"Layla." She bundled the cloth and cup in her hands before standing. "Yours?"

Telling her my real name was a dangerous move. I hadn't even told those hunters. Surely by now, word of the attack had reached town. If any other hunters had survived, they might look for me. Or maybe the wolf pack tortured information out of them, so they could identify all those involved. I wouldn't put it past them. I'd seen what a feral pack of wolves was capable of.

The least Layla knew about me, the safer I was.

But...the thought of lying to her, even though I barely knew her, made my chest feel heavy. For the first time in years, I wanted to be honest. Step out of the shadows. If only with my name.

"Wyatt."

With a slight nod, Layla rounded the couch.

I relaxed and stretched out my legs. From this position, I could better see the cabin's layout. A small kitchen was off to one side where Layla stood grabbing something out of the fridge, and a narrow, wooden staircase wound up to a second level.

I twisted toward her, but the sharp pain in my stomach diverted me back to front and center. "How long was I out?"

"The remainder of the night and most of the next day. It took a lot to control the bleeding." She wandered back into the living room and offered me a bowl. "It's broth. You need something in your stomach."

Someone banged on the front door.

Layla sucked in a sharp breath as her wide gaze shot to the door. "Damn it," she muttered.

My pulse spiked. Being in a stranger's home was risky enough without someone else figuring out who I was. "Are you expecting—"

She shook her head, holding a finger over her lips shooshing me. *Huh.* My angel didn't want anyone to know I was here. Interesting. Although, she wasn't an angel...nor mine. So many wrong words in that one thought.

I nodded, following her lead. Not like I had much choice.

She placed the bowl on a nearby coffee table. At the door, she cleared her throat and shook her arms by her sides, seeming to compose herself. She unlatched the deadbolt and opened the door wide enough to speak through the gap.

"Oh, hey, Trey."

A guy. Why that knowledge caused the muscles in my jaw to twitch was irrelevant. I only hoped this dude didn't know her well. I'd just met her and even I could tell she was nervous by the high pitch of her voice.

"Can I come in?"

Hang on. That guy's voice sounded familiar. I racked my brain trying to place it, but I couldn't quite figure out where I knew him from.

Layla cleared her throat. "I was actually about to... take a bath. Is something wrong?"

Nervous and a terrible liar.

I shifted slightly on the couch, scooting closer to the edge.

"I wanted to make sure you were all right. You haven't been into town."

Layla's shoulders sank as she leaned against the door-frame. "I'm fine. I just need some time to myself, that's all."

There was a pause in the conversation where I wondered if the guy would ever get the hint to leave. Before the thought fully formed, wicked hunger clawed at my gut.

No, not now.

I folded at the waist, wrapping my arms around my middle as fever rushed through me. Dark blotches pulsed before my eyes. Nausea hit me like a fucking boulder, slamming into me so hard I toppled sideways, fell off the couch and banged my shoulder on the table.

"What was—"

"Oh," Layla squeaked. "I left the water running. I better go. Thanks for checking in. Bye."

I vaguely registered the door slamming shut.

My head throbbed as the pale amber veil overtook my vision. I retched, gagging on nothing but air.

Layla dropped to her knees beside me, pressing the back of her hand on my forehead. "Your temperature is the same. What's wrong? Is it pain?"

I grunted. Fire tore apart my insides, tightening the coil in my gut until it almost snapped. Layla disappeared and I reached for her—

Something sharp stabbed me. I blinked a few times at the needle sticking out from my upper arm.

"What...did you...do?"

My words felt thick and foreign. Dizziness swept over me, and I struggled to maintain consciousness.

Layla wrapped her arms around my shoulders, easing me onto my side right there on the floor. "It will help with the pain."

No, it wouldn't. No human medicine would help. Only one thing cured the fire in my gut. Blood.

chapter three

Layla

I'm so stupid.

Why did I think this was a good idea? That saving a hunter would be okay? A hunter. In my home. I almost burst into hysterical laughter.

As the pain meds kicked in, Wyatt dozed on and off. Father was going to kill me. After he killed Wyatt. I could see it now—a blood bath of epic proportions rivaling what had happened in the woods last night. He'd never forgive me for saving an enemy, but I couldn't let Wyatt die. The war between shifters and hunters had gone on for too long. Centuries. It needed to end. And last night, I realized how badly I craved that peace. When I'd stepped in blood-stained dirt, coating the forest that was my home, I vowed to end the fighting.

How many more shifters would die because someone refused to take a stand?

When I found Wyatt lying there, barely breathing, I knew that person had to be me. I did the only thing I knew in my heart was right—I saved a life. Surely, Father would see it from my point of view once I explained the situation. If he let me explain.

I paced the room trying to figure out what to do next. From what I knew, without shifter blood, hunters healed like regular humans. Essentially, they were humans, well, witches cursed to crave shifter blood. If I could keep his cravings at bay with the use of pain meds and herbs, then we might both make it out of this alive.

I'd cleaned Wyatt's wounds, stitched them, and reapplied the dressing earlier this morning. I wasn't a doctor. I hadn't gone to a fancy medical school in the city, I was just a pack healer—a regular shifter who'd taken an interest in devouring healing knowledge from texts written by my ancestors. Usually, a shifter healed on their own, shifting back into human form until the magical properties in their blood did its thing. Provided the wounds weren't fatal, of course. But hunters? I had no idea if the shifter blood they consumed granted them healing properties, and if so, did they need to consume the blood regularly for it to work?

How long had it been since Wyatt digested blood? Was he running low? I shuddered thinking about it. I couldn't exactly cut open my vein and give him a boost.

He'd kill me.

He'd rip open my throat and drain my blood in two agonizing minutes.

I threw my hands in the air. Regardless of how I looked at it, my situation was screwed.

So, so screwed.

Pausing with my back to the fireplace, I looked at

Wyatt passed out on the floor. For a hunter, he was kind of cute. No, cute wasn't the right description and a strange word to associate with a hunter. With a strong, angled jaw dusted with dark stubble, and equally dark, broody eyebrows that furrowed even in his unconscious state, he seemed innocent, otherworldly. Mystical. I'd cut off his shredded shirt last night as I'd patched his wounds, and now I couldn't stop staring at his smooth, tanned torso —his strong, thick shoulders, the deep grooves beneath his defined pecs, his rippled abs, and the sinful trail of black hair that disappeared under the open button of his jeans.

I swallowed as a slight quiver trembled in my belly.

The sooner this guy left the better. Saving a hunter because I wanted peace was one thing. Fantasizing about said hunter while he lay unconscious on my floor was entirely different. Inappropriate. Reckless even. And a long list of other words to describe a situation so dangerous I couldn't have even dreamed it.

Another knock on the front door made me jump.

I groaned. I hardly ever had visitors when I stayed out here, and the one time I harbored an injured enemy, everyone came knocking.

I unlocked the deadbolt and eased the door open enough to speak through a small gap. Baker stood on the other side with hands stuffed in his pockets.

"Hey. I wasn't sure if you'd be in the bath already."

"Huh?"

He frowned. "I passed Trey on the way here, and he said you were about to have a bath and not to bother you. Which of course, I didn't listen to because I refuse to let that dumbass boss me around even if he is your father's overseer."

I totally forgot about that lie. I really needed to get it together.

"Just grabbing wine. You know, to have in the bath."

His gaze narrowed, reminding me again of how well he knew me.

"Or you're just full of shit and told him that so he'd leave you in peace."

I tried to plaster on a convincing smile, but Baker saw straight threw it.

"Lay...what's going on?"

"I...ah..." My gaze instinctively shot to Wyatt on my living room floor. I couldn't lie to Baker, even if I wanted to. He was my best friend. We'd always had each other's back. But even though I'd known him since birth, I wasn't sure how he'd react. Actually, that wasn't true. I knew exactly how he'd react. He'd totally lose it before rolling up his sleeves and asking what I needed him to help with. That last thought convinced me to tell him...well, part of the story.

I snagged the front of his shirt and yanked him inside, closing and locking the door behind him.

Baker glared at the body on my floor. "Did you kill a human? Because, Lay, I'm done burying bodies this week."

I almost corrected him until I remembered that we couldn't sense a hunter unless they were in bloodlust rage. Full hunter mode. Unconscious, Wyatt smelled like an ordinary human with a slight difference that I hoped Baker didn't sense because he was too focused on whether I'd killed someone. If I kept him distracted enough, Baker would never know.

"He's not dead."

Baker stepped forward, but I grabbed his arm, redirecting him to the kitchen. Farther away from Wyatt meant less chance of him discovering I harbored an enemy.

"The guy was caught in the crossfire last night, I found him barely alive beneath my porch."

Baker frowned, reminding me again that he wasn't an idiot. I steadied my breath so my heartrate calmed down a notch. I also called on whatever gods would listen to make sure Wyatt didn't wake while Baker was in my cabin.

Imagine the catastrophe that would cause.

"How did you get him inside?"

I leaned my hip against the counter. "With great difficulty."

More than that. It had taken every ounce of strength to haul Wyatt up the porch stairs. It wouldn't surprise me if the poor guy had bruises on his back from me.

"Why didn't you call me?"

I sensed the hurt in Baker's voice as well as a hint of suspicion. Rightly so. Our bond was thicker than blood. It was almost unheard of that I would partake in a reckless endeavor without him by my side. Growing up, I didn't have a single memory that didn't have him in it.

"It all happened so fast. I found him, managed to slow the bleeding, and then he's been in and out ever since."

Baker wasn't convinced. The way he tilted his head and searched my eyes was a dead giveaway.

"I don't like you staying out here alone with an injured stray. Who knows what he's capable of?"

I snorted, motioning to Wyatt. "Does he look dangerous?"

Spoiler alert: he was more dangerous than Baker, but I kept that to myself.

Baker didn't say anything for the longest time. "I'll go grab some clothes and stay here with you until he's well enough to leave."

Damn protective wolves.

"Actually, I need you to keep Trey away. The last thing I need is him finding out and running to my father."

Father usually called before he visited. He probably feared turning up at my home to find a naked man in my living room. *Yeah, right.* If only he knew I hadn't had a man in my bed for what felt like forever.

Baker's mouth twisted as he thought it over. "Layla..."

He only ever called me by my full name when I proposed a bad idea and he wanted to talk me out of it. Which hardly ever worked. Except for that time when... wait, I needed to stay focused.

I playfully punched him in the arm. "Are you doubting my badass fighting skills?"

He barked a laugh. "I'm not dumb enough to underestimate you. The last time I did that was in sixth grade, and you busted my nose."

I grinned, remembering the one and only time he'd called me a chicken.

"All right." He huffed. "But I want a text from you on the hour, every hour until the guy leaves."

"Really? That's a little—"

"No text and I'll kick down your door."

I glared at him. The hard set of his bearded jaw told me he was serious, and I was all out of arguments. Fine. If sending a text was what I needed to do until Wyatt healed enough to leave, then I'd do it. My heart needed this. *I* needed this.

I nodded.

"Every hour."

I shoved him toward the door. "I get it. Now go!"

When Baker left, I leaned against the closed door and took a deep breath. All I wanted was to save a life. Prevent more death. But in doing so, my yearning for peace could be the one thing that destroyed my pack.

chapter four

Wyatt

I peeled open my eyes in the same room as last time—on the floor in the cozy cabin. Only now, my platinum-haired angel paced back and forth between me and the fireplace. With her hands on her shapely hips and her head bowed, staring at the floor, she hadn't noticed I was awake. I took the reprieve to figure out more about her. Like, how the hell she'd dragged me inside? Did she have help? How much did she know about the hidden world surrounding her? Not that I could answer that by staring at her back.

Since I blacked out, she'd tied her hair in a messy heap atop her head, giving me an uninterrupted view of her slender, creamy neck. Necks were my weakness, always had been. Even before I'd become fixated on a particular jugular. That just took my fascination to the next level. Instead of fantasizing about what it would feel like to trail my fingers along her soft neck, I switched my focus, dragging my gaze lower.

Layla pulled a cell phone from her back pocket and

held it in front of her. My pulse spiked. I couldn't see whether she stared at it or sent a text, but she didn't hold it up to her ear for a call, so that was a relief. Kind of. No one called these days.

Fuck.

My mind raced with more questions. Had she told someone she'd found a random dude in the forest? Was she updating them on my progress?

The last thing I remembered before I woke in this cabin was the fight with shifters and some asshole taking a chunk out of my side. If her cabin was nearby...maybe she knew about the shifter world. I was right in the middle of Timber Falls wolf territory. If she knew about the world, maybe she also knew about...shifters.

What if she was friendly with the local alpha? If she called someone from the pack?

Sure, having the alpha rock up at her door would save me hunting him down, but I was in no condition to fight, especially if more than one shifter accompanied him. They'd slaughter me before I even waved hello. Just like they had when they busted down Ellie's door.

I needed to get the hell out of here. I couldn't find a cure if I was dead.

Bracing one hand on the rug, I grunted as I pushed up into a sitting position.

Layla stopped pacing and spun toward me. "You're awake." Her words were kind, yet I caught conflict in her eyes. "How do you feel?"

"Better." Lies came so easy these days. At times, even I believed them. "How long was I out this time?"

"The night." She glanced at the cell again, her brows furrowed as though considering something.

"Are you expecting a call?"

Her chest rose with a deep inhale before she slipped the cell back into her pocket. "No. I..."

The same determination I'd seen when she found me darkened her pretty eyes. I couldn't stop looking at them as though the glacier pools lured me in with only a fleeting glance.

Big, big trouble right there.

"You can't stay here much longer."

I plastered on my best cocky grin. "Why? Will your boyfriend come knocking again?"

She shot me a deadly glare. "That's none of your business. You're only here until you recover."

Such feistiness from a tiny human.

I held up one hand. "Fine. I got it."

I expected nothing more. Who in their right mind would rescue a stranger in the woods and let them recover in their cabin...alone?

Settled in a seated position, I assessed my stomach wound. The pain had dimmed but only a notch, no doubt thanks to whatever she injected me with before I passed out. But the surrounding skin burned like a hot iron. Healing would take longer than I anticipated. To speed it up, I needed some old-fashioned remedies, which a few rare herbs could provide. But to do that, I had to figure out how much she knew then somehow convince her I wasn't the bad guy. I couldn't exactly wander outside and search for the herbs on my own.

I bent one knee which lessened some of the pain. "Are you a doctor or something?"

"Or something."

She handed me a glass of water, and I gulped down the contents before cursing to myself. I'd already placed a dangerous amount of trust in her without even realizing. Like now, she could've poisoned me, and I might be seconds away from an agonizing death. I placed the empty glass beside me and braced for a reaction, dizziness or a wave of nausea that never came.

Huh. Maybe she was just a strange, young lady living in the forest surrounded by ferocious wolves instead of a hoard of pet cats.

"You're pretty cagy for a woman healing a random guy she found in the forest."

She huffed. "You know what? I hate small talk more than I hate summer and that's saying something. So, now that you're coherent, why don't you tell me why the heck you were under my back porch?"

I drew back. "Right. Straight to the point. I like it."

"I don't care what you like. I only care that you don't die on my watch."

I cocked a brow. What crawled up her ass while I was unconscious on her floor? Had I drooled on her priceless rug? "I was in the woods and...ran into a bear."

"Except, bears don't roam in Timber Falls."

I shrugged one shoulder. "Maybe this one was a loner?"

She crouched before me, and a hint of peonies swept through the air. If only she didn't smell so goddamn good and kept distracting me. Once I healed, I had to refocus on finding that cure, and I couldn't worry about her running interference.

She lowered her voice to barely above a whisper. "I know what you are, Wyatt."

My heart stalled. Not who, what.

Playing dumb was the best I could manage. I wouldn't confirm a damn thing until I knew we were on the same page. Humans knowing about my world wasn't unheard of, but it also wasn't common. My luck she was one of those.

I plastered on my cocky grin again, the one that always got me out of trouble. "I don't know what you're talking about, sweetheart."

She rolled her eyes, and it sent a blast of heat through my middle. The good tingly kind, not the painful kind. What was it with this woman?

"Remember when I said I hate small talk? I also hate lies. Admit it. You're a hunter."

I stared into her eyes searching for a hint she was bluffing. If she knew about the shifter world, she most likely knew about hunters, too. It made sense. But how the hell did she know I was a hunter? Since last night—or the night before? What day was it?— I hadn't flipped into bloodlust rage...well, except for right before she stabbed me with that syringe.

She must've seen my eyes before she jabbed me, even though I didn't think I'd transitioned that far. Regardless, her knowing made things easier.

I lifted my chin. "Perfect. Now we've got that awkward conversation out of the way we can get to know each other."

"You're not denying it? Trying to convince me you're *not* a bloodthirsty killer?"

I shrugged. "What's the point? You said you don't like lies. Besides, I'm not ashamed of what I am."

Not really. Most of the time.

Her brows shot up. "Huh."

"My turn. How do you know about hunters? Are you friendly with the local pack?"

Her gaze darted to the door and back. "Something like that."

I lowered my voice and smirked. "Not exactly an answer, sweetheart."

She stood, putting distance between us. Did I make her nervous? Was she worried I'd bite? I'd only do that if she were a shifter, and I'd already established she wasn't.

Determination once again settled on her features, tightening around her mouth. "Listen, let's skip the get to know each other part, the less we know, the better. Once you're healed, you can leave."

I couldn't argue with that. "Fine with me."

She motioned to the dressing over my stomach. "Let me take a look."

I leaned back and peeled the gauze aside way too slowly for comfort. That sticky stuff hurt like a bitch coming off. Underneath, a big angry wound scowled back at me. I wasn't a doctor, but even I could tell that the long, festering slashes across my stomach hadn't healed. That black-tinged skin looked gross.

Using a pad, Layla smeared a white substance over the tears in my flesh. Her gentle touch awakened something primal, deep within me. An instinct to...protect?

33

How ridiculous. Only one woman ever needed my protection, and I'd failed.

Layla leaned closer, inspecting the wound and once again, her soft floral scent consumed my senses. It drifted through my nose, curling around my lungs before seeping into my blood. A feeling so familiar yet so...strange.

This woman was bad news. I needed to heal and get the holy hotness out of there.

But...what if Layla knew more than she admitted? That wouldn't surprise me. I knew more than I'd told her. If she knew the supernatural world, maybe she even knew a shifter or two. That would be...convenient. If she'd spent time with the alpha, she'd know where he lived. That would be even handier and would save me a shit load of time. She could lead me right to his doorstep. Except for how she muddled my senses, spending time with her wouldn't be a hardship.

Sudden giddiness tingled in my chest. I could finally end this. I could find the cure and finish what Ellie started all those years ago.

After changing the dressing, Layla sat back on her haunches with a deep frown. "It's still not healing. I've tried everything, but it's not making any difference. I've never treated a...hunter before. Is there something else that will accelerate your healing?"

When her face paled, I knew exactly what thought popped into her head. Blood. Shifter blood was the quickest way to heal any wound, but for hunters, it came with risks. Lately, I'd balanced on a knife's edge between digesting blood to stall the cravings and full-on I'm-going-to-rip-your-throat-apart bloodlust. Even the mention of blood made my stomach tighten.

Bracing my forearms on the couch behind my back, I heaved myself off the floor. Only, I never made it to my feet. Instead, I collapsed on the couch, landing on my side. I gritted my teeth as stabbing pain shot through my stomach. Layla was right, the wound wasn't healing, and I didn't have time to wait. The wound wouldn't kill me, hopefully, but being this incapacitated put me at risk. Even more so if Layla knew the pack. One of them might drop in for a visit and serve me up for dinner.

I moved into a more comfortable position. Besides blood, one other thing could help. "There's an herbal paste that accelerates healing, but the ingredients aren't easy to come by."

She straightened her shoulders. Such fire. A pang tightened my chest, but I brushed it aside. I couldn't let emotions cloud my judgment. They'd gotten me into this mess, but they had no place in my future.

"I know someone who has access to herbs." She slipped the cell from her pocket, thumbs at the ready. "Which ones do you need?"

I rattled off the herbs and precise instructions on mixing them as she jotted it down. Her thumbs paused as she looked up at me through the longest dark lashes. "I suppose a witch needs to mix it? Or can you?"

For a human, she sure knew a lot. This wounded, I didn't have the strength to access my magic, otherwise I would've found the herbs and healed myself. But I wasn't sure how I felt about admitting that weakness to her.

If I had more energy, I would've slapped my forehead. She already knew the extent of my injury; I couldn't even get off the fucking couch. Every minute in this state put me in more danger.

I gave a slight shake of my head.

All witches knew simple healing incantations, they were usually the first lessons taught. Though, the spell's success depended on the witch's power. But at this point, I'd accept anything.

"Okay. I'll be back as soon as I can." She grabbed keys and her coat, pulling it on. At the door, she glanced over her shoulder. "Oh, and, Wyatt, I'd stay inside if I were you. Wolves prowl these woods, not bears."

chapter five

Layla

Layla: *Road trip to Woodland Falls?*

I shot a text to Baker before starting the car and driving through the forest, heading into Timber Falls. Two seconds later, he replied. Poor guy seemed glued to his phone ever since he found out about my situation at the cabin.

Baker: *Sure.*

Baker's family lived on the outskirts of the pack's territory, on a large plot of land that backed up to an adjoining forest with my family. As pups, Baker and I played in the shared forest, spending endless days battling imaginary hunters. Even back then, I yearned for peace, and Baker always won.

Some things never changed.

As I neared his family's drive, I slowed the car and spotted him standing beside a tree at the edge of the road, half concealed by shadows.

He jumped in the passenger side. "That human recovered yet?"

I snorted, accelerating back onto the road leading to Woodland Falls. "Are you sure you're not my older brother rather than my cousin?"

He side-eyed me.

I sighed. "Honestly, the wound isn't healing. I thought Mia could mix a concoction that might help."

Thankfully, Baker didn't ask how I came up with that idea. Although Baker usually handled the liaison with other packs, it wasn't unheard of for the alpha, or next in line for alpha in this case, to pay a visit. Plus, Mia and I had become friends since she mated with Noah.

"Or you could seek permission from your father to use blood."

Shifters rarely used their blood to heal humans. The side effects were too unpredictable. Sometimes it worked, other times it sent the human on a wicked bender which had, on more than one occasion, almost led to the discovery of our existence. No wonder my father, along with the other alphas, prohibited it.

Besides, Wyatt was a hunter, not a human. Giving him my blood could cost me my life.

"I want to try the paste first."

Satisfied, Baker turned up the music, and I pretended this was an ordinary road trip with my best friend. One where I didn't have an injured hunter hiding in my cabin. Or one where I wasn't harboring a pile of secrets from those I loved.

One where the sting of betrayal didn't slowly eat away at my soul.

A few hours later, we pulled up outside the Whitcome house in Woodland Falls. A sweeping two-story farmhouse with a wrap-around porch, and cute open shutters on the windows. Mia and Noah had slowly renovated it back to its original glory.

Inhaling a deep breath, I exited the car and followed the path up to the porch.

Mia opened the door before I reached it. "Hey, Layla. Good to see you again, Baker. If I'd known you were coming, I would've made some lunch." Her face twisted in a grimace. "Though, my cooking skills are fairly basic."

I pulled her in for a hug. "Actually, I'm hoping you can help me with something witchy."

"Always. Come on in." Mia held open the door for me and addressed Baker. "Noah just left to open the bar if you need to see him."

Baker glanced to me as though silently asking if I needed him to stay. I didn't. Mia had so many wards on this place, no one with ill intent could venture near it again.

I tossed Baker the keys. "Say hi for me."

Baker headed back to the car, and I followed Mia inside to the kitchen.

"Can I get you something? Tea? Something stronger?"

I shook my head. "Just water thanks. I drank too much soda in the car on the way here."

Mia laughed, filling a glass before passing it to me. "What witchy business can I help you with?"

I unlocked my cell and showed her the list. "I wondered if you could make a healing paste using these herbs."

Her expression softened as she read it. "I heard about the attack in Timber Falls. Ash said it was a bloodbath."

I swallowed the bile rising in my throat. "That's an understatement."

"Were these herbs in the grimoire I gave your father? They're different to the ones I use."

Damn it. All the lies. For someone who hated them, I'd sure told my fair share in the last twenty-four hours.

I nodded, which was no better than lying with words.

Mia poured herself a glass of water, and I slipped my cell back into my pocket.

"According to my grandmother's notes, that grimoire belonged to an original family, so I'm sure the herbs are legitimate. I assume shifter blood hasn't worked?"

Shifter blood rarely failed, so I needed to tell her the truth. "Actually, the injured person isn't a shifter."

"Right." She peered at the roof as though mentally checking off a list. "I have everything except the black sage, but I know where I can get some. We don't need much. How urgent is it?"

I almost laughed. I needed that concoction and Wyatt out of my cabin yesterday. Scrap that, I needed to never find him beneath my back porch in the first place. But that didn't happen. I did find him, and now I needed him to heal as quickly as possible so he could leave, and all the lies could stop.

"Urgent."

Mia reached for her cell on the counter. "I'll make a call."

As dusk settled, painting the sky in rich, vibrant swirls of pink, Baker and I arrived back in Timber Falls. Instead of dropping him at his place, he insisted on coming with me to my cabin and brushed off my arguments as though they were specks of dirt on his jeans.

On the way through town, I detoured to the local store to stock up on groceries while Baker waited in the car. I had no idea how long it would take for Wyatt to heal or if the paste would even work, so I bought enough food to last another week just in case.

With grocery bags loaded in both hands, I returned to the car just as my phone rang.

Baker grabbed bags from me as I answered the call.

"Hi, Father." I paused next to the car. "How are the injured shifters?"

Not going to the infirmary this morning caused a knot in my belly. I'd been too focused on healing the enemy. How messed up was that?

"They'll all make a full recovery, thanks to you."

Baker took the remaining bags and loaded them into the trunk.

"Listen, I just wanted to make sure you were back. I spoke to Ashton Cole earlier, and he said you and Baker were in Woodland Falls today."

Heaviness pressed on my chest. One of these days, likely soon, all this deceit would burn a hole in my soul. If it hadn't already.

I rounded the car to the driver's side. "Yeah, I... wanted to stock up on a healing paste that Mia made. In case there's another attack."

In case healing hunters became a regular thing. I rolled my eyes at the absurd thought.

"Good idea. With a hunter potentially unaccounted for, we need to prepare for another attack."

I stumbled, almost dropping my phone. "What? A hunter unaccounted for? But I thought Trey said we caught them all."

Baker slammed the trunk and gave me a wide-eyed look.

My father mistook the hitch in my voice for fear. I wasn't afraid of a missing hunter. The hunter wasn't missing, he was hiding in my cabin.

"Trey can't be sure whether he counted four or five. Given the mayhem, I don't blame him." His voice softened to the fatherly tone I'd heard so many times before. "We're safe, Layla. I have a group searching the woods as we speak."

What? Ice-cold chills skated down my spine. What if they heard someone inside my cabin while I wasn't home? What if Wyatt had another episode, and the wolves sensed a hunter nearby? What if he ventured outside and attacked the wolves? They'd kill him.

Could this situation get any worse?

"Is Baker still with you?"

"Yep." I swallowed, glancing over the car at Baker as my skin tingled.

"Give him the heads up. And stay alert."

"I will."

The second I hung up my brain kicked into action. I jumped in the car and started the engine. Baker barely made it into the passenger side before I skidded down the road toward my cabin.

"What the hell's going on?" Baker braced his forearm on the door as I screamed around a bend.

"I have to get back. They suspect there's a hunter still out there. They're searching the forest right now."

I gulped, trying to steady my breathing. Dread sank heavily in my belly as we entered the forest and I hoped like hell for once the wolves hadn't found their target.

"What does that have to do with your cabin?"

"He's the..."

I sucked in a sharp breath. *Shit*. I'd almost told him.

Baker's stare burned a hole in the side of my head, but I kept my gaze firmly on the dirt road, giving my brain time to come up with another half-truth. Something I could tell him that wasn't a lie.

But I couldn't do it. Digging a hole, pretending everything was okay wasn't helpful to anyone. I needed to confide in someone, but once Baker knew, he'd have to keep my secret. Once I said it, I couldn't take it back. That wasn't fair to him. He didn't ask for this, he didn't tell me to save a hunter. I did that all on my own. This was my fault. I refused to drag him down to hell with me.

"Layla? Why are you in such a rush to get back to the human?"

I shook my head, trying desperately to focus on the road and not hit a damn tree.

"Slow down before you kill us."

Tears filled my eyes, and I took my foot off the gas, stopping the car in the middle of the road like a crazy lunatic.

Baker twisted to face me, his brows drawn. I'd never seen him more worried, not even when we lost our way in the network of caves at the foot of the mountain when we were eleven.

He softened his voice. "Tell me. It can't be that bad."

I choked out a laugh, holding back the flood of tears. "Oh, you have no idea."

"Whatever it is, Lay, I have your back. You know that."

When I turned to him, the trust and faith reflected in his deep blue eyes undid me. Telling him was the right thing to do. I couldn't lie to my best friend.

A tear slid down my cheek as an invisible force squeezed my heart. "He's not human. I saved a...hunter."

chapter six

Wyatt

I managed to lift myself off the couch and somehow made it to the small bathroom to take care of business. Thank the stars a bathroom was on the ground floor. No way in hell could I have made it up that narrow staircase without faceplanting and tumbling back down. Afterward, I stumbled to the couch completely fucking exhausted.

Probably thanks to the infection slowly eating my insides and how without my magic, I healed like a fragile human. And given I ran a little low on blood.

I peered at the covered window in the living room as light faded around the edges of the drapes. Layla had been gone for hours. All day. Where the hotness was she? Surely it didn't take that long to find a witch and a few herbs. Rare herbs, but that was beside the point.

What if something had happened to her? Why the fuck did I even care? My concern for her whereabouts came from the need to heal, it had nothing to do with the tingles her soft fingers left on my stomach or how her vibrant eyes drew me in until I forgot my own goddamn name.

Get a grip.

I cursed, forcing my gaze to the ceiling so I stopped side-eying the door, hoping she'd stroll through. More was at stake than my precious ego. If Layla didn't come through with the healing paste, I could kiss this life goodbye. Everything I'd done, every choice I'd made, would've been for nothing. I didn't have the time nor the inclination to screw around with a human. Too many lives were at risk for me to fail.

And so far, I'd done only that.

After fluffing the pillow harder than it deserved, I shuffled farther down the couch and lay on my back staring at the exposed rafters.

A branch snapped outside.

I jerked upright and instantly regretted it. Fire ripped through my side. Grunting, I swung my legs around to sit cradling my stomach. I fought through the pain, clenching my jaw, and angled my ear to outside.

Silence.

Maybe I'd imagined it. Maybe I'd fallen into that mystical place between wakefulness and dreaming, only to call forth pain-induced hallucinations. Wouldn't be the first time. And with my mind so focused on the searing heat burning inside me, I had no hope of detecting an intruder. I was as good as an ordinary human in more ways than one.

Just as I convinced myself I was crazy, yet again, boots thumped up the porch stairs at the front of the cabin. Not Layla, her steps were softer, lighter.

The person knocked on the door.

Damn it.

I looked for a place to hide but getting there in time was the issue. Whoever was on the other side of the door must've suspected Layla was home. Probably because the fucking lamp was on and the fire lit.

Still cradling my stomach, I quietly stood, half bent over and shuffled toward the downstairs bathroom.

The person knocked again. "Layla?"

I paused mid-step. That voice again. I recognized it. The dude who'd come to check on her yesterday...or the day before.

What was his name? Trent? Todd?

Turd?

Diverting to the fireplace, I slid out a poker from the holder just in case the persistent dropkick barged in. I couldn't take him on without a weapon. Even then, it may not make a difference.

When everything went quiet, I relaxed a little, leaning my shoulder against the wall thinking the guy made a sensible choice and left. Until a key slid into the lock.

Fuck.

"Trey?" Layla's voice called from somewhere out front.

"Hey. I was just about to—"

"Use my spare key to go inside my cabin?"

Smart girl. *Kick that dickwad in the balls and be done with him.*

I inched closer to the door, still gripping the poker,

listening to the conversation I had no right to overhear. Though, I'd love to know his excuse.

"You got me." The idiot laughed. "I was worried something had happened because the light was on, but when I knocked, and you didn't answer."

Not that you gave it time.

There was a long pause before Layla spoke. "Baker and I ducked into town. I guess I left it on by mistake. Did you need something?"

"Only to make sure you're okay. I smelled blood on your back porch."

First off, when did he search the back porch? Second, why hadn't I heard him? What kind of guy crept around someone else's porch when they weren't home? And third, that creep spoke of blood as though he wasn't human. Was he a shifter?

Did Layla know?

"There was a lot of bloodshed, I'm not surprised some ended up there," another male voice chimed in, one I didn't recognize.

I snuck to the window and peeked through the gap between the drapes. One guy stood with his back to me by the front door. Layla stood on the top step with the other guy behind her. I couldn't see enough without pulling back the drape and making it obvious.

"I don't recognize the scent of the blood. If we missed one, he might still be out there."

Heat flashed through my body. Missing? Had the others figured out I was alive and kind of kicking?

Layla's brows shot up. "He? How do you know the missing hunter is male?"

"I don't." Turd shrugged. "Rhett has organized patrols, so whoever it is, we'll find them."

Patrols? He had to be a shifter. But if that were the case, I should've sensed them. Unless my injuries affected my sense of smell, too.

I resisted the urge to tap the window and wave. *I'm right here, asshole.*

The guy behind Layla pulled off his baseball cap to ruffle his hair, but I still couldn't see his face clearly. "Who's on patrol tonight?"

Even from inside the cabin, I sensed the absence of love between those two males. But I was too stuck on how familiar Layla was with them. We needed to have a chat. She knew more about the supernatural world than she'd admitted.

"Just me on this side of the reservation," Douchebag answered.

Layla gave the second guy a sideways glance. "You should help."

"Nope. We have a lot of things to...discuss."

She waved a hand in the air. "That can wait. It's not as important as helping Trey search the far side of the reservation."

She stepped onto the porch, and I lowered the drape, leaning the fire poker upright against the wall. Crisis averted.

"Besides," Layla said. "A hunter wouldn't return here. Not with wolves in the surrounding forest."

I almost laughed. My angel was fiery and funny. What a seductive combination.

My. There I went again. Lots of things wrong with

that statement, but I had more important matters to consider.

"Layla...we need to discuss the thing we talked about," baseball cap guy said, his voice a little too stern for my liking.

Layla opened the door slightly and replied, but I didn't catch it. Wicked pain shot through me, twisting my stomach.

No, not now.

I backed away from the door. It hit me so damn fast. Blood. Shifter blood. The small rational part of me that still clung to humanity mentally scanned for the source of the blood.

Close. So close. Not enough to consume me, but it wouldn't take much more.

"Is that your blood on my doorframe, Trey?" Layla's voice speared through the haze, snapping my attention to the door.

"Yeah, sorry. I jogged around a tree and a branch cut my shoulder. It's already healed."

Trent. Trey. I didn't give a fuck about his name. He was a shifter. Layla knew about my world because the scumbag who tried to break into her house was a fucking shifter.

"C'mon, man. Let's go hunt a hunter," the other dude called out.

I gritted my teeth, gravitating closer to the door.

Blood. I needed it. I craved it. But I couldn't let myself flip, not with them so close.

That asshole had about ten seconds to flee before I lost control and bloodlust overtook my actions. Given his shitty manners, and my desperate need to heal, I doubted I'd hold back.

Nor would I feel bad for draining every ounce.

My fingers trailed along the wall as I prowled closer to the door. The conversation on the porch faded into the background. Saliva welled in my mouth while wicked tightness gnawed my gut. My pulse slowed as other more dominant senses fired to life. The scent of shifter blood lingered in each inhale as though I bathed in it.

Soon, I'd take my fill.

It wouldn't cure me, but it would hold off the cravings until I found the alpha.

Amber flashed in my vision, pulsing in time with my thudding heartbeat. My gums ached, pushing my canines lower. I fought to suppress the feral growl building in my throat.

Bloodlust took over and this time, I surrendered to it.

A hazy figure slipped inside the cabin. I ran my tongue along the sharp edge of my fangs, sending a heated shiver along my spine. The second the door closed, I slammed their back against the wall, immobilizing their hands above their head. I gripped the throat, angling the head to better access the neck. My favorite vein. The one with the biggest and fastest rush.

Baring my fangs, I lowered my mouth to the delicate flesh, ready to strike—

The scent of peonies swept through the air, overpowering my thirst for blood, stirring a different need.

Layla.

Somehow, through the bloodlust, I registered her, pinned between me and the wall. Heat swirled between us, fueling a more pressing ache as she trembled beneath my grip. The amber swarming my vision gradually retreated as her features came into focus. Her long hair twisted around my fist. Her rapid pulse.

I had no idea where the shifter ran off to, and I didn't care. My plans suddenly took a sharp detour.

At her neck, I licked a trail along her soft skin all the way to her ear. "I want so badly to sink my fangs into your pretty neck. Right here, right now."

Layla shivered. Not entirely the reaction I expected, given I could drain her life in three seconds.

Drinking human blood was pointless. It gave me zero power and did nothing to heal my wounds. Though, I'd bet her blood tasted as delicious as her scent. I bet it was the closest thing to heaven I'd ever experience.

When the bloodlust retreated enough to regain full control, another scent slammed into my senses, burning my tongue.

Fear.

Usually, I thrived on it, but...*Layla*.

I recoiled, staggering backward.

"Fuck. I'm sor—"

Her arm swung out, punching my side.

"Argh." I grunted, folding at the waist as sharp stabs ripped through my stomach.

Layla shoved my shoulders, and I stumbled back. "I've saved your life twice now and you repay me by trying to...drink my blood?"

A dull ache moved into my chest, clawing my lungs. She was right. I'd just attacked her in her own home after she'd saved me.

"I'm...sorry."

Dizziness swept over me from the stabbing pain in my side, and I grabbed the back of a chair to remain upright.

"Now, if you're finished, I have groceries to unload."

With a huff, she stormed back outside. For a human, that woman had one hell of a punch. It still vibrated in my bones.

Once the pain ebbed, and I regained my breath, I hobbled to the kitchen and sank onto a stool. Layla returned with grocery bags and unpacked them in silence.

"I'm sorry, Layla, I really am. I didn't mean to...I smelled shifter blood and lost control."

Not the first time.

She paused, a can of pasta sauce in her hand, but didn't say anything. What could she say? She wasn't the one who'd done anything wrong. That was all me.

I lifted my chin. "Where'd the loser go who tried to break into your house?"

Given the glare she gave me, any moment now, I half expected fire to puff from her nostrils. "Why? So, you can drain his blood instead?"

"No." Another lie, but whatever.

I straightened which stretched the gauze, only to slouch again. "Why does a shifter keep showing up at your door, Layla?"

She braced her hands on the counter staring me down. "Listen. While Trey is out there, looking for you I might add, you're stuck here. You can't leave, otherwise, he'll kill you." Her mouth twisted. "Control the hunter.

I'm risking a lot by saving you, and even more by hiding you in my home."

A sour taste filled the back of my throat, and I ran a hand through my hair. "I didn't mean to..."

She cocked a brow. "Try to eat me?"

I couldn't hold back the smirk. "Oh, sweetheart, if you want me to eat you, all you have to do is ask."

She scoffed, but the heat in her vibrant blue eyes betrayed her. It seemed we were both expert liars.

Hang on, maybe this could work in my favor. Given I was stuck here until I healed enough to fight back, I'd use her friendly connections with the local pack to get closer to the alpha. Return to my original plan. A strange knot tightened my gut overshadowing the pain, but I pushed it down. More than my life was at stake here. Though, if she regularly dealt with jackasses like that shifter, then I had my work cut out for me.

I was the biggest asshole of them all.

chapter seven

Layla

Baker texted me for the millionth time. At one point, I thought he'd turn up on the porch and bust down my door. I owed him big time for distracting Trey earlier and pretending to patrol with him to make sure he didn't return here. Keeping my secret was a lot to ask, and if we didn't both want peace so badly, he wouldn't do it. He'd kick my ass. But ever since we'd begun to understand the war, and the lives it destroyed, we'd both wanted it to end.

Though, that didn't mean he'd forgive me so easily for hiding a hunter in my home without telling him.

After unpacking the groceries, I sent him another text, reassuring him everything was fine. I glanced into the living room to find Wyatt by the fire, his arm braced on the mantle, his back to me. He still hadn't put a shirt on. Okay, he didn't have one, a wolf had shredded it when they tried to kill him, but that was beside the point. After I'd stopped the bleeding, I bundled the remains of his destroyed clothes with the bloodied gauzes and towels and tossed them in the fire. I couldn't add it to my trash. Hunter blood was unmistakable. A wolf would sniff it out a mile away.

Thank goodness Baker left spare clothes here for when he shifted, and they were a similar size. I could've bought Wyatt new clothes at the store, but someone would ask questions. Small-town gossip was the worst, and would no doubt create a world of problems I couldn't deal with right now.

So, here he was in my cabin, shirtless, with me staring at all his tanned bare skin and perfectly crafted shoulders. My gaze slipped lower following his spine, roaming over his muscular waist to stall on his perfect ass.

Shivers danced through my middle.

"If you keep looking at me like that, things are going to move in an entirely unexpected direction." He turned and my gaze collided with his. "Not unwanted, mind you. *Unexpected*."

"What?"

Oh, shit.

I'd openly stared at the poor guy for God knows how long. I probably had drool running down my chin.

He cocked a brow with that wicked grin curving at the corner of his mouth to reveal a sexy as hell dimple. "I have no problem with you ogling, sweetheart, but it's somewhat...distracting."

His gaze dipped to my mouth.

I swallowed down the flood of inappropriate thoughts. What the hell was wrong with me? It wasn't like I was sex deprived or something. Well, that wasn't exactly true. I was sex deprived, but totally content with the fantasies in my head right now rather than compli-cated relationships on top of pack expectations.

When my cheeks burned, I turned away, focusing on the glass jar Mia had given me. "So...how does this work?"

"First, we get naked, then a little kissing, touching..."

I spun, gaping at him.

He threw his head back and laughed, one hand cradling his stomach wound. "Oh, you meant the healing paste?"

If he weren't so injured, I'd punch him. Again.

"Of course, I did," I grumbled.

His golden eyes lit with a mischievous gleam, and I had the strangest feeling this guy could undo me in the worst possible way.

"My bad. I thought you were checking me out."

"I was not."

He gravitated closer, lowering his voice to a husky growl. "Sweetheart, you most definitely were. In fact, if those pretty blue eyes of yours held more heat, you'd incinerate us both."

I swallowed. How the hell could this guy see right through me? "Was not."

He held my gaze for a long moment, searching my eyes. Heat rippled through my middle, sparking an inten-sity I'd never experienced before. I had to keep reminding myself he was a hunter. Not a human. Definitely not a shifter.

"I thought you didn't like lies?" he murmured, much closer than a second ago.

Yes, I hated lies, but admitting my attraction to him,

to a hunter, was more dangerous. Whatever lust I felt for this guy would pass the second he healed and disappeared out that door. Engaging in fantasies with him was pointless. Our worlds would never align even if we somehow managed peace between our kinds.

I swiped the jar off the counter and held it between us. "How does the paste work?"

He took it, unscrewed the lid, and sniffed. "A witch made this?"

I nodded.

"Who?"

Even with the strange sense I could trust Wyatt, and the fact he hadn't done anything to make me feel unsafe —besides almost drinking my blood, which, in hindsight I still wasn't sure how I felt about—I couldn't tell him about Mia. Mia, the Whitcome witch, had been a topic of conversation around the packs ever since she'd somehow bypassed the hunter curse. She was also known for crafting a concoction that masked our shifter scent so hunters couldn't identify us from ordinary humans.

That concoction was probably the only reason I was alive right now.

I swallowed, lifting my chin. "I'd rather not say."

Wyatt considered me for a moment before nodding.

Crossing to the couch, he sat and stretched out his legs, placing the jar beside him. He pulled back the gauze. The red, festering wound looked as angry as the day before.

Using his fingers, Wyatt scooped out some dark green paste and smoothed it over his stitches. The second the paste touched his skin, it bubbled, sizzling like hot coals doused with cool water. Wyatt winced. Sweat beaded his forehead and after a few seconds, I couldn't watch any longer.

I knelt beside the couch, holding out my hand. "Let me do it."

He didn't argue.

With a sticky, thick glob on my fingertips, I looked up at him. "Ready?"

His Adam's apple bobbed as he nodded. He stretched out his legs farther, lengthening his torso, and tilted his head to one side so he could watch me. Something in his eyes didn't reflect only trust. No, the look he gave me was more...wonder. Curiosity.

Instead of deciphering why that made me feel all giddy, I focused on the wound. After three days, it still showed no sign of healing. Angry, red, infected flesh surrounded the claw marks, with dark purple bruising covering most of his stomach. Whoever did this had intended to kill him. How had he escaped? How had he made it to my porch? Did he kill the shifter who attacked him? If he'd taken a life in self-defense, did that make it okay?

God, I balanced on a dangerous edge. On one side, I almost felt relieved that he'd made it to safety, that I'd found him in time. On the other, the thought of him killing one of my pack sickened me.

If I wasn't careful, I'd fall on the wrong side and not be able to claw myself out.

Pushing all those thoughts aside for now, I smeared the paste on the first claw mark. Wyatt hissed a sharp breath, fisting a cushion.

"Does it sting or burn?"

He grunted. "Doesn't matter...keep going."

When I applied more, he winced again. His knuckles whitened, clenching the cushion, the muscles in his arm flexing. I hesitated. For all I knew, the paste was wrong and would do more harm than good.

"Layla." Agony seeped into his raspy voice. "I can... handle it. Keep going."

"But what if it doesn't work? What if it makes it worse? What if it's made wrong or I jotted down a wrong herb?"

He lifted a shaky hand and gently touched my cheek. "It's mixed right. I can feel it. It's the only option."

It wasn't the only option, we both knew that, but I refused to consider the alternative.

The sooner he healed, the sooner he left, and I could return to my pre-Wyatt life where my father groomed me for alpha and I fought a losing battle for peace. I wanted that, right? I peered into Wyatt's eyes as they bled between golden and amber, narrowing slightly as his hunter side fought for control. But his eyes didn't scare me, they held a fierceness that ignited something deep within me. I just didn't trust myself to acknowledge what it meant.

I scooped another blob of the paste and carefully smeared it over the other gouges in his flesh. The muscles beneath my fingertips clenched and unclenched as he grunted, but I kept going until I'd covered the entire wound.

Exhaling, I sat back on my haunches. "Now what?"

He took a long moment to answer. His eyelids

drooped as though he struggled to keep them open. "We wait to see...if it works."

If. I'd always hated that word. Someone should delete it from the dictionary.

"Okay."

A faint smile lifted the corner of his mouth as his eyes closed, and I sat there staring at him wondering how I'd gotten myself into this mess, and how the hell I'd get both of us out of it.

chapter eight

Wyatt

Her touch had branded me. That sounded impossible, ridiculous even, but I had no other way to describe it. When her fingers had smoothed along the claw marks over my stomach, something ancient awoke inside me. I hadn't experienced a sensation like that since...well, since I'd first tasted shifter blood and activated the hunter curse. But even the magnitude of triggering a curse was nothing in comparison to Layla's touch.

Opening my eyes, I lay there for a quiet moment assessing the tingling sensations as the healing paste did its thing causing my skin to buzz beneath the surface.

Although it seemed to work, the witch's powers lacked something. Skill or experience maybe. The witch Layla knew mustn't have practiced for long or wasn't far into her powers. Regardless, until I could fully access my own magic, I needed to shut up and make do.

I sank deeper into the couch as bolts of magic

collided with the faint hum of my own while my body slowly healed. In another few hours, overnight at most, I'd be up and about again. The sooner, the better. I needed to get what I came here for and end this for good.

I stared at the exposed beams in the ceiling for so long, lost in thought, that I didn't sense Layla until she parked her ass on the floor beside me. Cradling my middle, I sat up, making space for her on the couch. The movement not as painful as earlier.

"I'm good on the floor." From a tray beside her, she passed me a bowl and spoon. "Here, you need your strength."

Why the hell was she caring for me? I was a hunter. A bloodthirsty predator. If she truly knew about the supernatural world, she'd know how dangerous I was, especially in her home. Yet, instead, she fed me, tended to my wounds, and refrained from handing me my ass after I tried to drink her blood. I saw no hatred or disgust in her beautiful eyes, only compassion. With a hint of curiosity and...sass. Perhaps she had a bad boy complex. That thought made me grin.

"What's so funny?"

"Just trying to figure you out." I shrugged, accepting the bowl. "What's your deal with Troy?"

"Trey."

"Douchebag."

She chuckled and settled with her back against the coffee table, facing me. I dug into the soup, giving her the opportunity to reply. The idiot shifter and her obviously had history, and I wanted to know how far it went.

That thought terrified me more than facing an entire pack of wolves.

"You're persistent, aren't you?"

I shrugged again.

"We're...friends."

I called bullshit. "Sorry to be the one to tell you, sweetheart, but I don't think he got the friend zone message."

Her shoulders rose and fell in a heavy exhale. "We've known each other a long time. I guess over the years he expected we'd...become more."

A human and a shifter. Stranger things had happened. "Why don't you?"

She glared at me. "Not that it's any of your business, but we want different things from life. I've never felt that way about him." She dipped bread in her soup. "What's your story?"

"Oh, you know, an insane hunter with uncontrollable bloodlust." I winked at her, pretending for a split second they weren't the truest words I'd ever spoken.

She placed her bowl on the table and studied me. "Uncontrollable bloodlust? You seemed to control it when you..." She cleared her throat. "You know. I saw the switch in your eyes. You fought it."

I had. But little did she know, that was the first time I'd managed to halt the craving. Ever. Her scent had somehow broken through the haze, dragging me from the darkness with only a whisper. After years of trying every damn spell I found, I'd never even gotten close. Once the bloodlust took over, it didn't stop until the hunter side of me fed the inner beast, tearing through every shifter in the vicinity.

Layla remained quiet for some time, toying with the drawstring on her sweatpants. A big chunk of me wanted to know what troubled her so I could ease it. A smaller, much more logical part of me knew those feelings were too dangerous to explore. Feeling anything for this curious woman complicated things. It put a serious kink in my plan and wouldn't end my destructive cycle. Eventually, she'd see that.

I needed to keep my priorities straight. So, instead of asking what was on her mind, I kept my mouth shut, well, open, shoving as many nutrients in my body as possible. The quicker I healed, the better for everyone. Right?

"Why did you attack the pack?"

I stilled with the spoon at my mouth as my appetite crashed and burned in the fireplace. "You clearly know a lot about this world."

"More than you realize," she muttered.

I waited to see if she'd elaborate. Which, she didn't. "Are you sure you want that answer?"

Her gaze lifted to me, stirring that same weird sensation in my gut. Maybe the healing paste came with unusual side effects.

"I know hunters crave shifter blood, but do you...need it to survive? Is that why you attacked?"

Something sparked in her eyes, and I'd be damned if it wasn't heat. Had she...wanted me to bite her? No. Surely not. I'd sensed fear, yet...I shook my head, clearing those unhelpful thoughts. "What's with the questions?"

She shrugged. "Just curious. It's not every day I have a conversation with a hunter."

It also wasn't every day I had a conversation with a human who knew so much about my world. Sharing a little bit of information with her wouldn't hurt. In fact, it might aid in building trust. Then, maybe she'd return the favor and introduce me to the alpha.

I set my bowl on the tray. "Hunters crave shifter blood, yes, that's how it begins. But at some point, after years, the cravings switch to need. Blood becomes our sustenance, our lifeforce, it fuels our powers and strength."

"Powers?"

"And here I thought you knew everything."

She rolled her eyes at me, making me chuckle.

"Hunters were once witches. For some, those powers don't disappear after the change, and if managed correctly, they intensify with the use of shifter blood."

"If that's true, why don't you use your powers to heal yourself?"

I peered at the crackling flames. "Healing takes an incredible amount of power, plus the paste, and I was, am, too injured. Accessing my magic right now would drain me even more."

"But shifter blood would heal you."

She whispered it so quietly, I had to look at her to make sure she'd spoken.

Why did the idea of drinking shifter blood now make my stomach gag? "The paste will work fine."

Keep telling yourself that, man.

"Eventually, though, you'll need blood. You'll crave it again."

I held her gaze, trying to figure out why she wanted to know. Was it concern for the douchebag or the local pack? Or did she feel unsafe around me? And why the hell did any of that bother me?

"Eventually." I turned away. "But by then, I'll be long gone."

chapter nine

Layla

At some point during our conversation last night, Wyatt fell asleep again, curling up on his side on the couch. I'd draped a blanket over him, lingering for longer than I should've. I never imagined I'd save a hunter. Let alone, have one sleep in my cabin. Everything I knew, everything my ancestors had taught us now seemed slightly skewed. Hunters were evil villains, hellbent on killing shifters for their blood. I'd grown up with horror stories of battles and bloodlust, packs forced to hide for fear of hunters slaughtering their young.

Yet, when I stared at his face, his angled jaw covered with the beginnings of a short dark beard, his equally dark lashes framing his closed lids, and his slightly cracked bottom lip, I saw nothing resembling those monsters. I saw an injured man who'd done nothing to harm me. Sure, I'd seen him flip to his hunter instincts, but he'd also controlled them. He fought against them.

The stories never mentioned control.

Was the concoction I digested to mask my shifter scent so potent that even when in the same cabin with me, he still had no idea who, or rather what, I was? I hoped so. Because if Wyatt found out I was a shifter, particularly when he craved blood, I wasn't sure he could maintain control.

If he did though, it proved peace wasn't such a far-fetched idea. A step in the right direction.

In the kitchen, I quietly prepared some breakfast, going about my usual morning routine. Well, the routine I had before Wyatt found refuge under my back porch and flipped everything upside down. I'd had a conversation with Baker last night to put his mind at ease after he finished his fake patrol with Trey searching for the hunter who'd slept on my couch. It hadn't worked, but at least he'd agreed to wait until this morning to come over rather than the middle of the night.

I made myself a cup of tea and grabbed a firm green apple from the basket to slice.

I stole a glance at Wyatt, still peacefully asleep on the couch. What was his story? How did he trigger the curse? Did he have family? Were they hunters, too? Given how many hunters attacked Timber Falls, he clearly didn't travel alone. Were they his friends? Did hunters have friends?

A sharp sting made me hiss, and I dropped the knife on the cutting board.

"Shit."

Blood slid down my finger, dripping on the counter. Holding it upright, I reached for a cloth—

Wyatt's hand clenched my wrist. I hadn't even heard him move.

My whole body froze as he pinned me between him and the counter.

"This is a surprise." His deep, gravelly voice sent a shiver dancing down my spine. And not in a bad way, which concerned the hell out of me.

He moved closer until his body pressed flush against my back, his warm breath at my ear. My heart pounded, making me dizzy.

I couldn't even breathe.

When I moved to turn around, he braced his other hand on the counter, boxing me in.

This was bad. So very bad.

I should've listened to Baker.

Wyatt leaned forward, curling his arm around me, lifting my hand to his nose. Did he just smell my blood?

A deep groan rumbled through his chest. "I think someone has been lying."

"I...I can explain."

His chest rose and fell in harsh breaths. The heat from his body seeped through my shirt. I wished I could see his eyes, to know whether he was in control. To know which part of him spoke to me right now—Wyatt or the hunter?

My pulse skipped as he angled his head, trailing his nose along the side of my neck, inhaling another deep breath. Every point where his body touched mine blazed, threatening to incinerate me. I couldn't tell whether the sensations zipping through me were good or bad.

Dangerous or...I couldn't even concentrate without seeing his eyes.

"You're a shifter," he murmured.

I needed to free myself from his hold, to spin around.

When I considered headbutting him, he leaned even closer and...placed a gentle kiss at the base of my neck.

A wild rush flooded through me. Heated shivers tingled along every nerve, stirring through my blood, pooling in one central place. A million butterflies fluttered in my belly.

Standing here was insane. More reckless than saving a hunter.

I should run.

His body curled around mine, wrapping me in his strong arms as his scent swept over me. Dark forests, cedar, and something spicy. I wanted to drown in it and never come up for air.

This was so wrong.

So dangerous.

Wyatt groaned, trailing his mouth up my neck to hover at my ear. "Your blood smells like a secret night garden in full bloom. Sweet, floral...luminous."

My knees buckled, and his arm tightened around my middle, holding me steady.

By now, the cut on my finger had healed, but a line of dried blood remained.

"I bet it tastes as sweet as it smells."

Oh, God. Someone help me.

The thought of him tasting my blood should repel me. It should disgust me. Yet, right this second, I almost...

craved it. I wanted to see his reaction as he licked my finger. I wanted to...feed him.

How sick was that? Someone needed to examine my head because it currently warred with my body, going back and forth. *Do it. Fight back. Surrender. Run.*

I sucked in a sharp breath when Wyatt's lips caught the fleshy part of my ear, transforming that simmer between my legs into a downright inferno. My eyes rolled back.

I shouldn't do this. Surrendering to these feelings played with a fire I wasn't sure I knew how to extinguish. Or worse, one I didn't want to extinguish.

His growing hardness nudged against my lower back, adding fuel to the already out of control blaze. How could something so forbidden, so wrong, feel so...right?

Gently, Wyatt loosened his grip around my waist, and I took the opportunity to pivot in his embrace. He still held my wrist between us.

He lifted it to his mouth. "Let me taste you, Layla."

I could say no. His golden eyes, not yet thin amber slits, told me if I did, he wouldn't force me. I could also kick him in the balls and make a run for it. If I shifted, I could catch him by surprise and tear him to pieces.

But...I didn't want any of those things. Neither did my wolf apparently, who currently purred like a house cat lying by a window in the midday sun.

I'd never admit that aloud. Not even to Baker. This tiny error in judgment could remain between Wyatt and me. If I survived another day, no one else would know what we did. What I did.

Before commonsense kicked in, I urged my finger closer to his lips.

He stilled, inhaling a deep breath through his nostrils, his eyes flickering between deep gold and bright amber. "Watch me."

I could barely breathe, let alone watch. Watching made this...real.

"I won't hurt you."

I believed he wouldn't tear me apart, but I had a strange feeling that what fire lay between us would eventually destroy me. Destroy us.

My pulse thrashed in my ears, but I refused to close my eyes.

Holding my gaze, Wyatt leaned in and...licked my finger. I sucked in a sharp breath. Tentative at first, his tongue softly lapped at the tip where I'd cut it with the knife. He groaned. Heat flooded my core, rippling through me.

"So beautiful."

I couldn't speak. Could only watch, spellbound by his movements as his tongue licked from the bottom of my palm right to the tip of my finger, removing all the blood in one sinful stroke. I squeezed my thighs together as the intense ache soared to new heights.

So wrong. Yet, I never wanted him to stop.

When he captured my finger between his lips and sucked, my eyes slid closed, drowning in the bliss. Was it possible to orgasm without him even touching between my legs?

With that thought, things quickly turned a forbidden corner.

The space between us vanished with one step. Wyatt ground his erection against my middle, caging me between him and the counter. My free hand clutched the waistband of his jeans, holding him closer. Pleasure collided in a hot mess between my legs. I didn't know what I wanted, could barely think. All I knew was this man, his tongue, the downright sinful sounds coming from his chest, completely enthralled me.

Curling his tongue around my finger, he sucked in slow, purposeful motions. Each kiss careened me closer to that blissful peak until I thought my world would explode.

Something sharp scratched my finger, muddling my senses.

His fang.

Wyatt froze.

His hand tightened around my wrist. The low, dangerous rumble that vibrated in his chest sent an entirely different shiver over my nape.

Before I realized what happened, he recoiled, so fast he slammed against the wall on the opposite side of the kitchen. Cool air rushed between us, repelling the warmth.

Any residual pleasure vanished the second his eyes shifted into thin amber slits and locked on my finger. I looked down at the tiny scrape and fresh drop of blood.

"Run," he said between clenched teeth.

I stepped toward him. He'd controlled the bloodlust before, I'd seen it the night I found him under my porch and again last night when he smelled Trey's blood. "It's okay."

I reached for a towel.

The growl that came from his chest made the hairs along the back of my neck stand to attention. I stilled, arm outstretched and slowly looked over my shoulder at him.

The slits in his eyes had thinned even further until no white remained. Wyatt was no longer here. All hope of control died the second his fang cut my finger. Now, I stood facing a hunter who craved my blood.

"I said run," he shouted.

So, I did.

chapter ten

Layla

I bolted through the forest until my lungs burned. I didn't stop nor turn to see if Wyatt chased me, I ran for my life. Because I'd seen it in his eyes, the uncontrollable hunger burning within them. The look that told me he'd take my blood even if it killed me.

Just like every other hunter.

I dashed around a tree, following an unmarked path to town. To safety. A hunter wouldn't dare follow.

I slammed into someone, tripping over, faceplanting on the ground.

"Holy shit." A guy loomed over me, and it took a few seconds for my brain to catch up and identify Baker. He offered a hand, helping me off the ground. "What the hell are you running from?"

"I..." I bent at the waist, taking a few moments to catch my breath and figure out what to tell him. I couldn't tell him I ran from Wyatt because he'd ask what happened, and then I'd have to tell him I was stupid enough to let a hunter taste my blood.

What an idiot.

I dusted the dirt from my knees. "Nothing. I was... running, yes, but from nothing. Jogging, you know, for exercise."

"Bullshit. For starters, you're wearing jeans." He studied me, the expression on his face tightening around his jaw. "Did the hunter hurt you?"

He twisted in the direction of my cabin, but I snagged his arm. "No. I just...I freaked out a little that's all."

Baker cocked a brow, clearly not convinced. "Since when do you freak out?"

Since I let a hunter taste my blood.

I seriously needed my head examined.

"Why are you here?" I asked, changing the subject.

"I texted you and said I'd swing by before the pack meeting."

In the...excitement, I'd totally forgotten about the text. My stomach twisted. What if Baker had seen what I'd done? What if he'd shown up when Wyatt was in hunter mode?

"Is he healed? Did the paste work? 'Cause I don't like the idea of you alone out here with a hunter in your cabin."

I shushed him. "Keep your voice down." I lowered my own. "Yes, the paste seems to have worked."

Wyatt looked healed to me, though I didn't get a chance to check his wounds while I was too busy turning into a gooey mess with his mouth at my neck.

"Good," Baker grumbled. "So, he's gone then?"

"I'm sure he will be by the time I get back."

Wyatt wouldn't stick around now, not when we'd

crossed an ancient line we should've stayed miles away from.

I ignored the sting in my chest and hooked my arm in Baker's. "Come on, we have a pack meeting to get to."

Avoidance was the key, and I was an expert.

Baker tried his best for small talk, and I nodded and contributed at all the right times to avoid further questions. By the time we made it to my family home, I'd mostly calmed down. Though, I couldn't stop my thoughts from wandering back to Wyatt. Had he left? Was he completely healed now? Was he okay?

Would he be there when I returned?

That last thought confused me the most. I shouldn't care, I shouldn't have saved him in the first place, but something had compelled me. More than my hope for peace, more than my need to cease the bloodshed between our kinds. A strange connection had pulled me to him. I didn't know if he felt it too, and I still didn't understand it, but every time I caught him looking at me, or when we touched, something snagged in my chest. When I thought of how my body reacted the moment he'd licked my finger, I almost collapsed right there on the porch.

Pushing the thoughts aside, Baker and I headed through the entrance to the large open room at the rear of the house roughly the size of a grand ballroom. My father used this space for pack meetings. Chairs were set up around the room, and most of the pack were already there. I greeted them as I weaved through the bodies, finding a seat near the front.

My father gave me a smile that said, "It's good to have

you home." Only, I wasn't staying. Though, maybe I should. Returning to my cabin after what Wyatt...what Wyatt and I did, made a million critters take flight in my belly.

He'd tasted my blood. I'd let a hunter taste my blood.

Why did I want him to do it again?

Had I lived such a boring life that I needed to rebel in my late twenties? Thinking of his tongue as it circled around my finger, his lips sucking on the tip, made my freaking toes curl.

Bad, bad idea. Back to avoidance.

I crossed my legs, twisting in the seat. Baker dropped in the seat beside me as my father cleared his throat. Noise in the room hushed as the pack gave him their full attention. Except Trey. Trey stood on the far wall, focused on something else. I leaned forward slightly to find out who he was looking at, but couldn't quite see without falling off my chair.

"Thank you for coming on such short notice."

I straightened and Baker gave me a weird frown.

"Since the attack on pack land, I've been in contact with the neighboring towns," my father continued. "It seems the group of hunters targeted a few smaller communities before hitting Timber Falls."

"Before we handed them their asses," someone hollered from behind me.

"Before we killed those fuckers," someone else added.

My stomach churned as cheers erupted.

My father motioned with his hands for them to quiet. "We did. But it's not over yet. From reports, it seems there were six hunters. Not five as we first thought."

My mouth went dry. They had proof of a missing hunter, not just Trey's word. The butterflies I had earlier morphed into creepy crawlies eating away at my insides.

"Perhaps the hunter came to their senses and fled, but we all know if that happened, they won't be gone for long. Once they have the thirst for blood, they'll return to finish what they started."

Murmurs and whispers sounded around me, but I barely heard them as my pulse whooshed in my ears.

"What's the plan?" someone asked.

I leaned forward, bracing my forearms on my thighs taking deep breaths.

"Effective immediately, I'm enacting patrols of the surrounding woodlands. I also encourage you and your families to be inside your homes before dark. Hunters rarely attack during daylight, they're creatures of the night. Until we find them, stay alert. I've organized a fresh batch of masking elixir, now is not the time to run low." My father paused, waiting for the news to sink in. "Any questions?"

I couldn't concentrate on the discussion around me. They knew another hunter was out there, that one had survived. I sucked in sharp breaths. What would they do if they knew I saved that hunter?

Tingles erupted over my cheeks. Blackness dotted my vision.

I was about to puke on my shoes, right there in front of the entire pack.

A male crouched in front of me, and I vaguely registered my father. "Layla, are you all right?"

I was so sick of people asking me that. As though at any second, I'd fall apart.

I'd done this. I saved a hunter, put our pack at risk, made families fear for their safety.

Wyatt's soft whispers repeated in my mind. I couldn't imagine him killing a shifter. How could someone so gentle turn into a monster?

He told you to run...

"Layla?"

I shook my head, clearing the thoughts. "I'm fine, Father. A little unnerved, that's all."

He patted my knee. "Don't worry, we'll catch the hunter."

Exactly what I was afraid of.

After the pack meeting, I ditched Baker for the bookstore. Not being a reader, he didn't fight it, and I couldn't get out of there fast enough.

I all but burst through the bookstore door and sighed as it closed behind me. Safety and security, surrounded by fictional worlds.

I couldn't believe what had just happened. My father wasn't stupid, he'd hunt the missing hunter until he was dead and buried on pack lands as a warning to others who sought to attack us.

Wyatt. He'd hunt down Wyatt.

Oh, God. I'd tipped over the edge. I sympathized with a hunter. Someone who sought to...drink my blood. More importantly, why did that cause a stir in my belly?

Why didn't I tell my father? Why keep this a secret? At any time during the meeting, I could've stood up and told them I knew where the missing hunter was.

In my cabin.

On my couch.

Licking my blood.

I shook my hands, trying to rid the energy and weird sensations firing through my body as I ascended the metal staircase, venturing to the rear section of historical romances. I trailed my fingers over the spines searching for a book that spoke to me.

He told me to run. Yet, all I could think about was going back to make sure he was okay.

Hiding in the bookstore for an hour wouldn't solve anything, but I didn't care. I needed to clear my head and figure out what to do next. In here, I could pretend for a moment that I wasn't betraying my father, or my pack, by harboring the enemy in my home. I could pretend I hadn't made a huge error in judgment.

Rough hands landed on my hips. I squealed.

"Shh."

Wyatt.

I spun to face him with his cocky grin, and those damn dimples. Why? Why the dimples? As if his smile weren't enough to swoon over, his face had to add an extra layer of sin in the form of twin dimples.

"You scared the crap out of me," I whispered to him. I grabbed the sleeve of his shirt tugging him farther into the corner. "You shouldn't be here. Wait a minute...how did you know I was here?"

That grin deepened. In these moments, he didn't

resemble a hunter, or a bloodthirsty killer. He looked like an ordinary guy who happened to lick my...

"My blood," I murmured to myself. "You tracked my blood."

He nodded. "Handy, don't you agree?"

Huh. I wasn't so sure about that. Obviously, his witchy powers were back online.

I let go of his shirt and gave him a once over, searching for scratches, lingering far too long on his muscular arms. "You're healed."

The corners of his mouth kicked up. "Thanks to you." He jerked his chin at the books behind me. "Don't tell me you're one of those hopeless romantics who believes in happily ever afters."

I scowled at him, so over people making fun of the romance genre. "Yes, I am. I believe in fated mates and finding that one person you're meant to be with. The other half of your soul." I lifted my brows. "Don't tell me you don't believe in love."

Something flashed across his face too quick to catch. "I didn't say that."

I studied him more closely now that he wasn't lying half-dead on my couch. I had to admit, he was easy on the eyes—tall enough that I could snuggle comfortably under his arm, but not feel as though he was a giant. Strong, broad shoulders. Not as wide in the shoulders as Baker, taller and leaner, but still as built. His striking jawline looked even more chiseled now that he'd healed. How was that possible?

He'd also changed into a dark pair of designer jeans with a black T-shirt that fit him better than Baker's. Had he stashed spare clothes somewhere before the hunters attacked Timber Falls? Regardless, no amount of clothing stopped me from remembering the firm, ripped torso that hid underneath.

"Would you prefer I take my shirt off?"

"What?"

His grin widened as though he knew exactly where my thoughts had gone. Damn him.

I cleared my throat. "Why are you here?"

Ever so lightly, he trailed the back of his finger along my jaw, moving down my neck to pause at my thumping pulse. "We need to talk."

I swallowed. How could he ignite such a reaction? He'd barely touched me, yet my body was on fire again.

"About what?"

I played dumb, it was the best course of action. *Avoid, avoid, avoid.*

Gazing into his glimmering gold eyes, I once again struggled to imagine him as a hunter.

His thumb swept over that spot on my neck. "The fact that you hid what you are from me."

Somehow, through the brain fog, I found my voice. "Do you blame me?" I lowered it to a whisper. "You're a bloodthirsty hunter."

He leaned down so we were eye level and so, so close. "And you're a beautiful shifter."

He'd said it. I hadn't imagined it.

I was a shifter. He was a hunter. He craved my blood. Which was probably why his thumb gently stroked the side of my neck.

Wait a second...he called me beautiful.

I stepped back, and he lowered his arm.

"You can't be here. The pack knows there were six hunters. They know you're still out there."

He shrugged.

I gaped at him. "They're looking for you."

"Let them."

Was he serious?

The bell chimed downstairs as the bookstore door opened.

"Why aren't you concerned? You're healed. You should leave before they find you."

His hand reached for me again but stopped midway. "They can't scent me when I'm in control. And they can't see me now I have some magic back." He stepped closer. "We need to talk."

Were all hunters this cocky? Or was it a witch thing? Was it just a Wyatt trait?

I lifted my chin. "What if I don't want to talk?"

One dimple decided at that moment to make an appearance and steal my attention. "Oh, I think you have as many questions as I do."

"Layla? Are you still here?"

I jumped as the bookstore owner called from the bottom of the stairs. I darted from behind the stacks and peered over the railing. "I'm here."

My breath punched in and out. One of these days, someone would catch me with Wyatt and unravel all my lies.

"I'm about to close up. Are you almost finished?"

I'd been here way longer than I thought. "Sorry, I totally lost track of time."

"Don't rush." Kelly waved a hand in the air. "I still have a few things to do."

"Okay, I'll be right down."

I turned back, but Wyatt had gone, leaving nothing but an open window and lingering warmth where his fingers had touched my rapid pulse.

chapter eleven

Wyatt

I curled my lip, sneering at the overprotective wolf loitering in the forest outside Layla's cabin as though she couldn't protect herself. Not that the wolf saw me. Layla had spent the past few days with a hunter in her home. Idiot. I was pretty sure she could look after herself and didn't need an entourage in the forest.

I darted between the trees with more stealth than that wolf could ever hope for. I felt good. Strong. A buzz still lingered in my blood, reinvigorating my magic. And I couldn't figure out what was responsible for the boost. The healing paste or the tiny drop of Layla's blood?

Though, given how quickly the paste worked, I was wrong earlier. The witch who made it was clearly from a powerful line, most likely one of the original families. I'd tried to keep track of them over the years, but when the bloodlust became too much, priorities shifted. For one, keeping myself alive moved up on the scale of important things.

I snuck around the back of Layla's cabin undetected thanks to the shadowy mist concealing me, double-checked for bodyguard shifters before using her spare key to slip in the door, easing it closed behind me. Yes, I grabbed the key before I left after our...moment. I won't apologize for taking the key. Nor did I care about sneaking in to wait for her.

Inside, I pocketed the key and made my way upstairs, pausing at the top when footsteps approached the front door.

"Night," Layla called out, probably to the dumbass wolves.

A howl replied as the front door opened.

She's with me now.

Layla closed the door and stilled with her hand on the knob. I watched her from the bedroom, wondering what bothered her. Me? I hadn't missed the way her pulse skipped in the bookstore when I'd touched her neck. Not out of fear, but another confusing emotion I didn't know how to comprehend. I for one, couldn't stop thinking about how her blood tasted. Like flowers drenched in pale moonlight. Yep. I'd reached the pinnacle of pathetic where I used fancy words to describe blood.

What the hell was wrong with me?

I backed into a shadowy corner, blending right in as Layla flipped on a lamp before ascending the stairs. Head down as though lost in thought, she didn't even notice me as she walked through the bedroom to the bath. I crept up behind her until she was within reach, then covered her mouth to muffle her squeal.

"Relax, sweetheart. It's me," I whispered in her ear.

Her body sank into my embrace, and something stalled in my chest.

Lowering my hand, I stepped back, giving her room to spin around.

"You scared the crap out of me again." She held her hand over her heart. "How do you do that?"

Somehow, I gravitated forward. As though my body couldn't stand being too far apart.

I frowned. "How do I scare you?"

"How are you so quiet and stealthy?"

"Magic." I leaned in, close enough to feel her breath tickle my lips. "How do you hide what you are?"

She huffed. "Okay. That's fair. Also, how did you get in here? The pack is all through the woods tonight. Some surrounding my cabin."

The thought of those wolves hovering over her stirred a strange heat through my gut.

"Oh, I saw them. But I told you they wouldn't see me. Besides, I felt having a little discussion with you was worth the risk."

She sighed as though not ready for the conversation but at the same time, knew it was inevitable. Me and her both. I was dying to know how she hid her true form from me. Even now, with a deep inhale all I scented was a human. Though, when I concentrated, there was a slight difference. Moonlight. She smelled like moonlight. Again, how did moonlight even smell? Regardless, the scent reminded me of a full moon, in the dead of night, drenching the earth in pale beams.

Kill me now.

"You're right. Okay." She motioned to the bedroom.

I gave her my best shocked gasp. "I dunno, we only just met."

She rolled her eyes. "So, we can talk."

Again, the dumbass insinuation was there.

I followed her back into the bedroom where she sank down on the corner of the bed. I relaxed in a reading chair trying not to think of the wolves outside plotting my death.

"Who are you?"

I cocked a brow. "That's the question you're leading with? I thought we'd already established names."

"I know your name, but who are you? Where are you from? What's your story?"

I crossed my leg, resting an ankle on my knee. "I thought we'd go question for question. My turn. Why did you lie to me?"

"Are you always this bossy?"

I couldn't stop my grin. This woman had the fire of a dragon, not a wolf. "That's three additional questions, sweetheart. I'm not sure you understand the concept of back and forth. Do you need me to explain it differently?"

She glared at me, and I barked a laugh.

"Fine. I didn't lie to you, I just...hid the truth. You're a hunter. I'm a shifter."

"And yet, you saved my life."

I took a moment to absorb that absurd statement. She had saved my life, the life of a hunter. A sworn enemy that craved her blood and that of all the shifters currently stalking through the forest outside her cabin.

She lifted her legs to sit cross-legged on the bed, toying with a thread on the blanket. "I...couldn't let you die."

"Why?"

I knew it was her turn to ask a question, not mine, but I needed the answer. For her to say it out loud. Maybe then, reality would hit me square in the jaw, and I'd wake up from this crazy dream.

She dipped her head and a loose strand of wispy hair fell over her face. The urge to tuck it behind her ear hit me so goddamn hard, I gripped the armrest to remain seated.

"I'm a pack healer."

I shifted in the chair, leaning forward. "But why did you heal *me*?"

"I've seen enough bloodshed for more than one lifetime." She lifted her gaze, searching my eyes. "Maybe it was reckless. No, it was definitely reckless, but I couldn't let you die."

I didn't remember much about when she found me. I had patchy visions of an angel appearing, preparing to take me to wherever it was I'd go after this world. But one memory was clear—the strange sense of familiarity I'd felt when she looked in my eyes. The determination. The way it reminded me so much of Ellie, my heart had split in two.

The same look she gave me now.

"I know it sounds weird, but I felt like if I let you die, a piece of my soul would, too. I've lost so many lives that, by now, I barely have any soul left."

That strange feeling tugged within my chest again. A

faint sensation I could easily shrug off as being in the same room as a shifter, but the more time I spent with her, the more it seemed different. Not a craving for blood. A deeper calling, one I couldn't quite identify.

"Thank you." I swallowed the lump forming in the back of my throat.

She fiddled with the loose thread again. "How did you become a hunter?"

A sour taste thickened in my mouth.

She'd shared something personal with me, it only seemed fair to return the gesture. Though, for so long, I'd wandered this earth alone on a destructive path with no end. I wasn't sure how to let someone else in. Many nights, I wished for the end. For the universe to take my soul. When I'd been near death beneath her porch, the weight lifted from my shoulders at the thought of no longer suffering.

Then, she'd saved me.

Her vibrant gaze captured me once again, and for a moment, I lost myself in the magic.

"I won't judge you."

A bitter laugh escaped me. "You say that now."

"Please...tell me."

Surely, she'd think differently of me if I told her the truth. Would she despise me for killing so many of her kind?

Regardless, I wanted to tell her. To finally let someone in.

"I had a sister once. Ellie. She had a thirst for adventure, but her witch powers were unparalleled." Once the flood gates opened, I couldn't stop. "The older she grew, the more she studied our ancestor's grimoires, honing her skill. Until one day, she discovered a grimoire full of dark magic and blood rituals involving...shifters. Combined with her powers, the mix was lethal. But as the darkness grew inside her, mixing with her newly triggered blood-lust, she became obsessed, stopping at nothing for more power."

Layla sat up straighter.

"I couldn't reason with her. The hunter curse consumed her more each day until I barely recognized her. Others began to notice." Bile rose in my throat. "Then one night while I was out...a pack of wolves targeted her, attacking our home. I wasn't there to..."

The words stalled.

"Oh my god."

I stared at the floor, my jaw tightening. "I retaliated the following night, killing several of the pack, and turned myself into the very same monster."

She was quiet for a long moment, and I lifted my gaze to gauge her thoughts.

"That's why you told me to run."

A shadow swept over her expression as though a war raged inside her head between her beliefs and the truth presented before her.

Maybe we weren't so different.

I drummed my fingers on the armrest, suddenly rest-less. "Bloodlust controls all hunters, but eventually, the need for blood consumes them. I don't want to..."

The sentence stuck in my throat.

Why had I told her to run?

I stared into her blue eyes, full of curiosity and...trust.

Realization surged through me. I'd never be satisfied with one fleeting encounter. I needed to know everything about her. And the more I thought about it, the greater that foreign urge to protect her surfaced.

She didn't need protecting, yet I still wanted that honor.

"You don't want to what?"

I met her steady gaze. "I don't want to hurt you."

Her breath hitched even though I suspected she knew why I'd told her to run. I'd lost control, gone beyond the point of return, and I needed her safe. I needed her away from the monster in me.

Before things got too sappy and I lowered to describing her moonlight scent, I changed the topic. "So, you live in this cabin on your own?"

Safer topics. Plus, I needed to know if there were any shifters out there with a target on their backs. A big, fat bullseye plastered there by me.

"Yes, I like it here. I like the independence and the solitude."

I smirked. "And the privacy so you can rescue injured hunters and keep them hostage without anyone knowing?"

She gaped at me, making me laugh.

"You're not a hostage. In fact, you should probably leave before they find you. Oh, God." She paused, the thread of cotton twisted so tight her fingertip turned red. "What if they find you in my cabin?"

"I'm just an ordinary guy...most of the time. Plus, I have a knack for hiding. Is it so rare for you to bring a dude home?"

A faint pink tinted her cheeks. "Yeah, it is."

"What about Douchebag?" I wouldn't mind stamping his forehead with the biggest bullseye.

"Especially not him."

Silence hung in the air while I processed what she'd confirmed. No mate. No boyfriend. Why did that send a happy little zip through me? I was in a world of trouble with this woman, and for some reason, I welcomed it with open arms and a cocky grin.

She straightened, unraveling the cotton from her finger. "Where will you go now that you're healed?"

I tilted my head studying her for a moment as clarity seeped in. "Actually, I think I'll stick around."

chapter twelve

Layla

The following night was my turn on patrol. My father had trained me from a young pup how to fight, and how to lead.

But tonight was no ordinary patrol.

With my father out of town, I led this patrol. This... fake patrol.

I stalked through the forest, a knife strapped to my hip, quietly treading over fallen branches. I'd gotten myself into this mess, and now I'd spend the night pretending to track a hunter when said hunter was safely tucked away in my cabin, probably lounging on my couch, and eating all my food. An invisible pull kept luring me back there. I didn't need to confirm he was still inside, I sensed it.

We'd talked for most of the night, but although conversation was easy, effortless, I was no closer to knowing why he attacked Timber Falls with the other hunters. Did that even matter anymore? Part of me hoped I could climb back over the edge to right myself, but the other knew that was a big, fat lie. At some point last night, I'd lost sight of the peak.

I smiled as I sensed Baker a moment before he fell in step beside me.

"Find anything?"

I shook my head. "I guess the hunter has moved on."

He side-eyed me. "Or he's holed up somewhere safe being cared for."

I bit my bottom lip, holding back a silly grin.

He sighed. "I thought you said he'd healed?"

"I did."

Baker flipped the blade in his hand, staring ahead. "I hope you know what you're doing, Lay."

Did I? A week ago, I never would've imagined being in this position. But when the paste healed Wyatt, I almost dreaded him leaving. I'd gotten myself into some dumb shit with my cousins growing up, but never anything to this extent.

"I can't shake this feeling..."

Baker stopped dead in his tracks. Even in the darkness, his wide eyes pinned me. "Please don't tell me you have feelings for him."

I frowned. Had I developed feelings for Wyatt?

Baker tilted his head. "Lay, you know what he is. End this before you get hurt."

Wise words, only I'd never been one to follow the sensible path. When everyone wore formal attire to Thanksgiving dinner, I wore an ugly Christmas sweater. When my father didn't roster me on patrols, I joined anyway.

When everyone killed hunters, I healed them.

But the pull to Wyatt was different than simply wanting peace. I felt drawn to him, even before he tasted my blood. When I'd found him injured under my porch, a strange sense of urgency had consumed me. I hadn't only felt compelled to heal him because of my role as a healer. Nor had I done it because I craved peace, although I told myself that. I sensed this fierce invisible tether extending from his soul to...mine.

I gasped.

A mate bond.

No.

He couldn't be.

He's a hunter...

"What's wrong?"

Before I answered, Trey cut through the trees. "The hunter is in the woods. Deakin spotted him about a mile north of here."

My heart flopped out of my chest and smacked the dirt. *No.*

"Let's go," Baker said, taking off after Trey.

All I could think of was how to get there before them. Would Baker pretend to hunt Wyatt like I did, or would he attack if he caught him? Why the hell did Wyatt leave the cabin when he knew a pack of wolves was looking for him? I'd told him to stay inside.

I'd kill him myself for making me run after him. He probably thought it was some fun game that we'd giggle about later.

Later.

Unconsciously, I already planned for later. For more time with him. Even more so now because I needed to know what our connection meant and if he felt it, too.

My heart raced as I bolted through the forest after Baker and Trey. In wolf form, I could track Wyatt better, but I'd lose my link to humanity, and I wasn't sure if my wolf would attack him or retain enough of my memories to know he wasn't the enemy.

There I went again removing his enemy status.

The only problem: Wyatt was an enemy to everyone else in this forest. Everyone except me.

Lungs burning from the foggy night air, I rounded a tree but skidded to a halt when Baker and Trey slowed up ahead. Hypersensitive, every minute sound pounded in my ears. I scanned the forest around me, doing a three-sixty. In human form, my vision wasn't as good, but it was enough. I'd spot him if he was here.

I slowed my breath, concentrating on that tether connecting—

Someone shouted from deeper in the forest. In one swift motion, Trey shifted. Clothes shredded, fluttering to the ground as his wolf darted between the trees heading toward the sound.

Baker spun to me, his gaze alert but wary. "Will he attack us?"

I shook my head, ninety-nine percent sure Wyatt wouldn't.

He told you to run...

A blur of movement caught my attention, off to the right. Baker noticed as well and ran toward it before I could stop him.

I had to get to Wyatt first.

Figuring Wyatt wouldn't draw attention to himself on purpose, I ran in the opposite direction, coming around in a circle. A branch snapped. I stilled. Imaginary fingernails scraped the back of my neck.

A hunter was close.

"Wyatt?" I whispered into the darkness.

Another blur whipped through the trees. Hunters had heightened senses and speed, and near immortality when digesting shifter blood. In human form, I was no match. Especially for a hunter who'd recently healed using a magical paste and...a drop or two of my blood.

Would the small amount make a difference?

Another wolf howled, echoing in the night.

My throat tightened.

I'd saved Wyatt only to have another pack member kill him. I couldn't let that happen.

I raced toward the sound. Bolting through the forest, I slipped half into wolf form, balancing on the edge, letting my vision sharpen.

An arm swung out, capturing my waist. My feet lifted off the ground. The world whirled.

I screamed, jamming my elbow into the ribs behind me.

Someone grunted but the hold around my waist tightened. "Relax, sweetheart."

Wyatt.

Why did he keep telling me to relax? Nothing about this situation was relaxing.

Air squeezed from my lungs, making me dizzy. Wyatt loosened his grip enough for me to turn around. "They're hunting you. Get out of here."

He shook his head. "Not me. There's another hunter in the woods."

What? Another hunter?

A wolf howled again, followed by responding howls. Had they noticed I hadn't shifted yet? That I was still in human form. Did they wonder why I wasn't responding?

"You need to get out of here. I need to shift, and I can't do that with you nearby."

Muscles popped in his jaw. "I'm not leaving you. Not until you're safe."

If I weren't so pumped full of adrenalin, I'd laugh. Not safe? He was a hunter. I wasn't safe with him.

Though, no part of me believed that.

Wyatt tugged me flush against him, backing us to a wide tree trunk.

He lowered his voice. "There's a traitor in your pack. A wolf working with hunters."

Bastard. That stung. "Labeling me a traitor isn't nice. Just because I—"

He frowned, looking down at me. "Not you, sweetheart. Another wolf."

"What?"

Wyatt cocked his head, listening. His lip curled. Fast, heavy footfalls caught my attention. Someone ran straight for us. Wolves howled again, closer this time. They were chasing someone, and that someone was about to find us.

Tremors wracked my body as my wolf fought to shift, the vibrations rattling through my bones. I couldn't risk it, not with Wyatt nearby. She might attack him.

I moved to step back, but Wyatt tightened his hold again.

"You have to get out of—"

Wyatt shoved me aside. I stumbled, the trees flipped. At the last second, I twisted, landing with a sickening smack. Pain seared through my leg where a broken stick plunged into my thigh. I gagged, easing it out and pressed my hand over the wound to stall the bleeding.

Wyatt grunted.

The thin amber slits of a vicious predator zeroed in on me from a few feet away. A hunter. Not Wyatt. Before I reacted, the hunter launched at me, fangs bared, but Wyatt was quicker. He leaped onto the hunter's back, arms locked around the hunter's neck.

Forgetting the blood oozing down my leg, I scrambled to my feet and unsheathed my knife.

The hunter stabbed a dagger into Wyatt's leg. He yelped, falling backward but reengaged just as fast. With a blade gripped tight in my hand, I searched for an opening as they fought.

Wolves howled, closer. The others were almost here. I needed to end this before they discovered Wyatt.

I darted forward. The other hunter snarled, swiping the knife at Wyatt. He leaped back as it narrowly missed his chest. Howls came from every direction, surrounding us. At least four different wolves closed in. I couldn't tell how close they were, or how much time I had left until a wolf attacked. If that happened, I'd have no choice but to shift.

The idea of fighting my own pack made me sick.

I flipped the blade, point down, and readied to strike the hunter. The hunter shoved Wyatt in the chest with such force, he flew backward, slamming into a tree. An inhuman snarl sent shivers down my spine.

It all happened so fast. The hunter lunged at me. I threw the dagger. A ghost-white wolf launched from between the trees. The hunter didn't stand a chance. My dagger slammed into the hunter's chest a second before Baker's wolf tore a massive hole in his throat. Blood spurted over me like a freaking sprinkler.

I gasped as the hunter thudded to the ground by my feet with Baker tearing at the flesh. Panicked, I turned to Wyatt. His thin amber eyes narrowed at Baker. His lip curled, revealing the tips of his fangs. His fists clenched and unclenched as though he struggled for control.

I had a split second to change the outcome. To get through to him before he attacked.

The scent of my blood and hunter's blood filled the air. Any second now, the other wolves would find us. If that happened, Wyatt would die.

He'd protected me, repaid me for saving him. If he hadn't shoved me away when he did, the hunter would've killed me.

When Wyatt's wild gaze darted to me, I whispered the first word that came to mind. The only one I knew would get through to him. "Run."

chapter thirteen

Wyatt

An amber haze distorted my vision. Blood consumed my thoughts as I sprinted through the forest, not hunting a shifter, but fleeing from one.

Layla. Her vibrant blue eyes flashed in my mind, clearing some of the fog.

A thin layer of sweat slipped down my spine as I ducked tree branches and fallen logs, using the last of my control to get far away. The sharp points of my fangs scraped my bottom lip, hungry for her. Craving her blood. Shudders rippled through my clenched muscles, tearing a path to the gnawing hunger curling in my gut. Tremors swept down my legs, but I pushed them harder.

With every step, I battled the all-consuming need to turn around. To sink my fangs into her pretty neck and bask in the taste of her moonlight.

One drop wasn't enough.

In the distance, wolves howled, their vicious snarls

echoing through the night as they ripped apart the other hunter. They wouldn't hurt Layla. She was safe.

I left her.

My feet faltered, needing to go back. To make sure she was safe. Protected.

Breaching the tree line, I stumbled, catching my balance before I faceplanted. I bent over at the waist, sucking in deep pulls through my clenched teeth. Bits of humanity fought with the bloodlust, fought for control of my mind. I couldn't go back. I knew without a doubt, she was safe. I needed to trust she could take care of herself. Wasn't that what I thought the other night? She didn't need a wolf entourage. She could manage on her own.

My breath steadied.

I should feel sorry for the hunter. One of my kind. A witch cursed into a life they didn't choose. A life they lived because of an ancient curse thrust upon them. But the hunter had attacked Layla. He was no friend of mine. If the wolf hadn't pounced on him, I'd have ripped the hunter apart for targeting her.

The amber in my vision receded a touch as I straightened, lifting my head. *Fuck.* Layla's cabin stared back at me. Unconsciously, I'd run here instead of the opposite direction.

Wolves howled far behind me, still no closer. At least they weren't chasing me. Not yet.

Layla.

My gut twisted as the hunger returned. Something had lured me to her cabin. A scent. Not shifter blood. Hers. Layla's. Those fucking midnight flowers I smelled every time I was near her.

My feet gravitated toward the door.

I battled with needing to make sure she was safe and doing what was right and getting as far away as possible. Again, she didn't need protection, yet I had a deep yearning to do exactly that. But I couldn't promise to protect her. I'd failed the one person who needed it the most.

Being near Layla put her at risk.

I stepped onto the porch as the amber film pulsed in my vision once more, demanding I submit. Taking control of my mind and actions. Desperate for blood.

I shoved open the door and stalked into the cabin.

This was more than a need to know she was safe.

I ached for her. I...craved her blood.

I'd saved her from the hunter. But now, who would save her from me?

chapter fourteen

Layla

In front of me, Baker shifted, returning to human form. Blood smeared his chin where he'd torn apart the hunter. I'd seen bloodshed, I'd seen hunters killed before. But this...

This could've been Wyatt.

Baker's wild blue gaze scanned me. "Are you hurt?"

I shook my head, unable to speak, still feeling lost and confused about what had happened. Wyatt had saved my life. He'd protected me.

What hunter saved a shifter?

Wyatt.

Baker rounded the gross remains of the hunter and placed a strong arm on my shoulder. "Are you sure? What the hell happened?"

I struggled to piece it together. Wyatt had pulled me from the chase, hiding me behind the tree as the hunter circled us. When the other hunter attacked, he'd fought to protect me.

"He...attacked. Came out of nowhere. I didn't have the time to shift."

"The hunter?" Baker sucked in a sharp breath, spinning to look at the gory mess smattered over the ground. "Fuck, Lay, was that your—"

"You got the bastard." Trey almost cheered as he strode toward us.

All I could do was stare as Wyatt's voice repeated in my mind.

A traitor in the pack.

Whoever it was put my entire pack at risk by engaging with the enemy. It could be anyone.

Oh, God.

Was I any better?

I couldn't stop the sense of relief flooding me. The pack caught who they thought was the missing hunter. Not Wyatt. He'd be safe.

How twisted was my loyalty?

I peered at the carnage. This was why I craved peace. This senseless killing needed to end. Wolves didn't kill with humanity; they tore apart their prey and feasted on their bones. This hunter had craved blood because he'd been cursed to do so, and Baker had slaughtered him for it.

When other wolves from our patrol darted into the clearing and shifted into human form, I checked my emotions, switching to autopilot. They couldn't know. Until I figured out who the traitor was, and what information they shared with the hunters, I needed to pretend nothing had changed. I mustered a flat, emotionless tone, and issued directives to bury the hunter's remains on the boundary and clean up the mess. Trey offered to report the attack to my father, but I declined, stating it should come from me. My father had headed to Cedar Valley earlier this evening to fortify our defenses. I didn't want him to freak out.

I needed to tell him about the attack, and the traitor. But first, I needed to find Wyatt and figure out what he knew. I needed proof.

As the adrenaline wore off, the sickening stench of blood and mangled flesh turned my stomach.

This could've been Wyatt.

"Report back once it's done," I demanded before I lost control of the tears threatening to stream down my face.

As I turned to walk away, Baker caught my gaze, a grim expression twisting his mouth. I slowly shook my head hoping he understood. They hadn't caught my hunter.

Not yet.

The wound in my thigh healed before I reached my cabin. I didn't know what compelled me to go back there, rather than search for Wyatt in the forest. I sensed him, a pull to him I couldn't ignore.

My mate.

I knew how ridiculous that sounded, but I couldn't deny it. The feeling that I'd known him all my life, the sense of awareness each time he glanced at me, the overwhelming need that had possessed me to save his life. It all pointed to a mate bond. My father had talked about it my entire life. How he'd scoured the world for my mom. I'd also seen the bond in other shifters and more recently, in Mia and Noah from Woodland Falls. A witch and a shifter. Their mate bond bridged the gap between two worlds.

In fleeting moments, like when Wyatt spoke to me last night or when he wrapped his arms around me, I felt that sense of...hope.

Maybe we weren't so unrealistic after all.

I pushed aside the strange heaviness in my chest. I needed to find him.

Dashing up the porch stairs, I slipped inside the cabin and locked the door. A low growl made me freeze. Slowly, I twisted. Wyatt skulked on the other side of the living room. In the darkness his amber eyes glowed, reminding me again he wasn't only my mate, but a predator who craved my blood.

His chest rose and fell in hard punches. I took a tentative step toward him. He growled, clenching and unclenching his fists.

I'd seen this side of him twice now. Once when he was too injured to hurt me, the other when he'd tasted a drop of my blood before pleading for me to run.

That seemed to be our thing.

One step toward each other, then run the other way.

This time, I wouldn't run.

I crept forward a step.

"Don't." His voice sounded feral, layered with a rawness that hadn't been there the other times. Had it?

I reached out my hand. "It's me. Layla."

His whole body rumbled with power, shaking his shoulders. With his knees slightly bent, arms tense by his sides, body angled, I recognized the attack stance all too well.

Would he attack me?

For a fleeting second, I remembered how far I was from town, from help, from my pack. If anything happened, if Wyatt lost control and attacked me, I'd only have my wolf to fight him off. Which was next to no help because every time I was near Wyatt, she purred and carried on inside my head as though she'd...found her mate.

The signs were there all along.

I had to get through to Wyatt. Did he feel the connection, too?

I stepped closer.

His feral gaze darted to my neck, and another shiver swept over me.

He craved blood. But without control, he could kill me. I had to keep reminding myself that even if he was my mate, he was still a hunter. Not a human, not a shifter. He was a lethal witch who'd activated a curse and now craved shifter blood to survive.

My blood.

His wild amber gaze dragged back up to my face as though struggling to fight the urge. I'd seen him control the bloodlust before, I'd seen him recover. I knew, deep down, he didn't want this.

Wyatt was still in there somewhere.

I took another step forward, now within his reach. My heart pounded, swishing in my ears. His lip curled up, revealing fangs. Another reminder of the danger. But my wolf hummed with energy. She didn't sense the urge to attack, to kill, or flee. She wanted more. More of him. That counted for something. I trusted her because at the end of the day, she was a part of me. She was me.

Now, I needed to trust Wyatt.

"Wyatt, it's me. You can control this."

I reached to touch his arm—

He snagged my wrist in a fierce grip.

I flinched, holding back a squeal. What the hell was I doing?

His gaze locked on my wrist. Not more than twenty minutes ago, this man had saved my life. He'd come for me, told me there was a traitor in my pack, and he'd fought the other hunter.

Even now, he held my wrist in an iron clasp and still fought for control of the bloodlust. What would it take to help him? To get through to him.

"Tell me what you need."

A feral sound rumbled from deep within his chest. "Blood."

He'd gone too far, last night he'd warned me this could happen. That when he lost control of the bloodlust, the only option was to feed. To sate the urges. I couldn't let him leave the cabin like this, some shifters were still in the forest, they'd sense him. They'd track him down and kill him.

They'd slaughter my mate.

My head told me to run. To scream, to raise the alarm, to flee from him and never look back. But my heart, the half of my soul connected to his, lifted my chin and kept my feet firmly planted on the floor in front of him.

I twisted my arm, turning the inside of my wrist up.

My heart either skipped or stopped beating altogether, I couldn't tell.

Although his eyes resembled that of a bloodthirsty hunter, I trusted Wyatt was inside there somewhere, that he wouldn't kill me. That he'd only take enough to quell the craving.

He'd saved me.

He trusted me to heal him, to care for him.

Last time, he'd told me to run.

With a deep breath, I lifted my arm, urging my wrist closer to his lips. His gaze shot back and forth between me and my wrist as though needing my consent. My permission.

My mouth was so dry the words came out all scratchy. "Take it."

His tongue darted out, licking the soft flesh on the underside of my wrist. A shiver of anticipation tingled through me, centering low in my belly. With his wild gaze watching me, he lifted my wrist toward his mouth, gently kissing it, then lapping at the skin.

The burning sensation in my belly intensified until my knees almost gave way from the heat building between my legs. And he hadn't even broken the skin.

I wanted him to bite me. I wanted it more than my next breath.

I trusted him.

"Take what you need," I whispered, urging my wrist closer.

My voice sounded foreign even to my own ears.

Wyatt growled again, that inhuman sound though this time it blended with a deep, gravelly moan. The wicked aching between my legs heightened.

Still watching me, his lips peeled back, and a sharp sting exploded in my wrist as his fangs punctured the skin.

chapter fifteen

Wyatt

Pale, warm light seeped into my veins. Gradually at first, then in deep, long pulls. Heaven. I'd never tasted something so intense. Each sip healed the slightest scratch, sealed wounds, blending with my blood as waves of power rippled through me.

With Layla's wrist in my hands, I sucked deep draws of her blood. Something powerful, ancient, flared to life. It pushed through the darkness, securing its claws within my soul before splintering it open.

Still, I kept my lips sealed over the puncture wounds.

Power and life. Something was different. Not ordinary shifter blood.

Moonlight.

Sweet midnight flowers.

The bloodlust haze lifted. As the need became less urgent, another sensation took over. A scent.

Layla.

The smell of her skin, her blood, drifted through my

nostrils, swirling inside me. Her wonder and amazement. Desire. Hot, raw, raging need.

No blood had ever tasted this divine. In the past, each time I lost control, I fed out of necessity to subdue the cravings. The thirst had become too much to bear, strengthening over the years until I no longer cared how much damage I inflicted with the bite.

I'd never taken the time to feed gently, to savor each drop. Now, I wanted it to last forever. I wanted to drown in her scent, her power, the life force fueling my strength as she fed me.

I heard someone. My name. I couldn't decipher the words, too lost in the blissful fog swirling through my mind. The world around me long gone.

A slight hitch in Layla's heart rate made my eyes shoot open. At some point, they'd closed. Her deep blue gaze stared back at me, slightly hooded, her lips parted with short panting breaths. Somehow, what had begun as a solution to the bloodlust, turned into something sensual.

"Wyatt..."

The desire in her voice sparked a wild frenzy in me. A need to have her. To take more than just her blood.

I backed her to the nearest wall, pressing her against it. Fire raged as my cock strained behind my jeans.

Her eyes widened. Alert.

"Stop."

I stilled.

Not fear, but concern trickled through her blood, jolting my brain back to life. I released the seal, drawing my head back as the twin puncture marks healed.

Still holding her wrist, I lowered her arm, rubbing my

thumb along the soft skin. Nothing had ever tasted so goddamn sweet. I wanted more, I wanted it every day for the rest of my existence.

"Are you..." My voice was too deep, too raw. "All right?"

She nodded. Her gaze dipped to my mouth.

The floor fell out from underneath me. I felt woozy, high on her blood, her scent, her taste. She watched me with so much heat, I figured I had two choices: step over the edge and explore the fire between us, or retreat.

Her pulse raced as though she battled with the same decision.

Not that it was a tough one.

Freeing her arm, I captured her face between my hands and peered down at her. Her hips rolled, pressing hard against my cock. I'd never considered drinking blood for pleasure, I didn't even know if other hunters experienced it. Her arousal rushed through our connection. Her need. And I was fucking here for it.

I shifted a leg between hers, parting them. She moaned, sinking into my body.

"Sweetheart, I want to do wicked things to you right now."

I slid one hand down her neck, over her fluttering pulse, further down her curvy waist to land on her hip. Her breath caught as I moved to cup between her legs. Heat burned through the fabric.

"More," she murmured. "I want more."

I slid my hand up and down the seam of her pants, and her head fell back against the wall.

"It's just the...blood. It makes you feel things."

One of us should be responsible.

"I don't care." Her lust-filled gaze locked on me. "If you don't put out this fire, I'm going to kill you."

I leaned in, trailing wet kisses over her jaw. "That'd be one hell of a way to die."

She moaned.

I popped the buttons on her pants and slipped a hand inside her panties. *Jesus.* The growl that came from my chest wasn't human. I didn't know what possessed me, but I couldn't control the need to devour her. When I circled my finger around her core, her hands grabbed the sides of my shirt, fisting the cotton.

I stroked her, imaging my tongue at her center, building her into a frenzy as her blood had done to me. She moaned, tilting her head to the side, and my breath stalled. I could sink my fangs into her neck, drink more of her heaven. Something told me she'd let me, that she wanted me to, but the need to pleasure her outweighed my yearning for blood.

Her breaths came harder, faster, and her legs buckled. Using my knee, I planted it between her legs holding her upright as I stroked. Her eyes slid closed.

"Open your eyes, sweetheart. Show me your pretty wolf."

When she reopened them, the pupils were dark and dangerous, and I saw the flicker of her wolf. It felt as though she battled not to shift and hand over control. With any other shifter, I'd brace for a fight, but with Layla, I sensed something more powerful. Something in her blood told me her wolf...accepted me.

Accepted this.

Accepted us.

I slipped my finger inside her heat, and Layla cried out, digging her nails into my sides. Nothing could top having her beautiful claw marks all over my back as I took her beneath me.

Her hands shifted to grip the back of my neck and yank my mouth to hers. Our lips crashed together. There were no gentle, delicate kisses, only raging need. My tongue tangled with hers in a battle for dominance, but I wasn't sure whether I wanted it, or wanted to surrender to it. I captured every sinful sound that came from her mouth spurring me on.

Her mouth tasted as heavenly as her blood.

I slipped another finger inside, filling her. When she nipped my lower lip and my blood mingled with the left-over taste of hers, the world turned fuzzy. In that moment, I wanted to fucking make her scream.

I pumped harder, sending her higher and higher, taking her mouth while filling her with my fingers. Her body stilled a split second before flying over the edge, scratching my shoulders as she cried out, tumbling over and over. I didn't relent, not until I drew every tremor from her, and she sagged into my embrace, breathless.

When her heart rate steadied, I eased back and stared down at the beautiful woman in my arms. Light pink dusted her cheeks, her eyes almost glowing an unnatural blue in the dimly lit cabin. How the hell had she captured my soul without me even knowing?

She smiled up at me, and something twisted in my

chest. It expanded, inflated. But as the lust fog faded, the reality of what just happened made my body tremble.

I drank her blood.

I lost control in the forest and used her blood to extinguish the bloodlust.

I *used* her.

Bile rose in my throat. "Fuck. I..."

I staggered back, fisting my hair. Chills raced through my limbs, chasing away the lingering warmth.

"It's okay." She stepped toward me. "I wanted you to. I offered."

Instead of protecting her, I'd put her in more danger. I could've killed her. If she hadn't stopped me, I might have drained her.

"I'm sorry. *Fuck.*"

I eyed the door.

I'd failed to protect Ellie. Eventually, I'd fail Layla, too.

My mouth twisted. "Why do you refuse to see me for what I am? I've killed shifters. Do you hear me? I didn't just drink their blood, I killed them."

Her eyes creased at the corners. "You became a hunter by avenging your sister's death. You're not the monster in this story, the wolves who killed her are."

"I didn't protect her, and now I'm putting you in danger," I snapped.

She moved into my space, placing her hand on my arm. "Wyatt, I'm okay."

I shook my head. This wasn't part of the plan. I needed to get the hell out of here before I hurt her. I inched toward the door, but a hidden anchor held me back. Leaving her while other hunters were out there, while she had a traitor in her pack, left her vulnerable. What was worse? Them or me?

She touched my cheek, softening her voice. "Don't leave. Stay."

chapter sixteen

Layla

Pain squeezed my chest as I watched Wyatt struggle with whatever thoughts raced around inside his head. Letting him take my blood, offering it to him, took whatever was between us to a whole new level, I knew that. But it also gave me more proof. He was my mate.

Without a doubt.

When his fangs had punctured my skin and took that first pull of blood, I felt nothing but the sharp pang of desire. A need to claim him, to make him mine. The yearning for him to claim me. And when I'd asked him to stop, he'd done exactly that. He hadn't fought me, hadn't caged me in without a choice.

Then...my legs trembled remembering what we'd done next.

"I should go."

His voice was raw as though he struggled to decide the right path, much like I had right before I realized he was my mate.

I reached for his hand, but he sidestepped. "I should've left the moment you healed me."

I drew closer again, not letting him retreat. "I think I know why you didn't."

A forceful bang at the door made me jump. *Oh, shit.* The attack. With everything that happened between us, I'd totally forgotten. Some next-in-line alpha I was, forgetting my duty because a drop-dead gorgeous hunter seduced me.

"Hide," I whispered to him, motioning upstairs.

Given he was back in control with the bloodlust at bay for now, whoever was at the door wouldn't sense a hunter. Hopefully, it also worked the other way. If a shifter was at the door, Wyatt wouldn't crave their blood.

Wyatt's body straightened, his jaw tight as his gaze shot between me and the door. For a second, I thought he'd argue, instead he darted upstairs, moving faster than I thought possible. Once he was out of sight, I adjusted my clothes and ran my fingers through my hair, so it didn't look like someone had well and truly screwed me against a wall. With my clothes on. Using only their fingers.

My cheeks flamed.

Nope. Think of something else.

At the door, I steadied my breath before opening it. Baker stood in the doorway. His eyes narrowed as his chest expanded with a deep inhale. My heart skipped. *Oh, God.* He could scent—

"Care to explain why you smell...different?"

Points for not actually stating what I smelled like. I

bet it was a mixture of arousal, blood, and Wyatt's alluring scent.

I opened the door wider for him to enter, quickly scanning outside for any other pack members loitering near my cabin. "We need to talk."

He'd been my favorite cousin and my best friend since we were pups. We never kept secrets from one another, but now, I felt so overcome by them I couldn't breathe.

"You're still seeing the hunter, aren't you?" Baker grumbled. "I think I'm going to need a drink to stop myself from killing someone."

I poured Baker a bourbon while I figured out where to start. Over the past week, I'd rescued a hunter, healed him, sensed a connection with him and then, let him drink my blood. And...I liked it. Oh, and said hunter gave me the most powerful orgasm I'd ever experienced, again, using only his fingers.

Umm, Baker didn't need to know that last part.

Before turning back to Baker, I quickly glanced upstairs but couldn't see Wyatt, even though his gaze heated the back of my neck.

Bourbon in hand, Baker studied me for a moment before taking a long sip.

I'd told my fair share of tales over the past week, and skirted around the dangerous truth, but I couldn't lie to my best friend. If I did, fate would lash out at me tenfold.

I tried to find the right words. "I..."

"Did he hurt you?" Baker's hand tightened around the glass.

I shook my head knowing he was totally serious. He

would murder a guy if he treated me badly, and he'd make it look like a hunting accident. Wyatt hadn't hurt me even though I'd given him all the opportunity. He'd been nothing but tender and compassionate, particularly when he'd drank my blood.

Stop thinking about it.

"No, he wouldn't hurt me. It's just...well, he's..."

I wiped my palms on my jeans. This was harder than I expected, I couldn't find the right words. I peered at the ceiling as though it would give me the answers, or at least a starting point. Baker stood there sipping his drink. He wouldn't press, I knew that, but I needed to get this right.

He frowned, and I could almost see the thoughts bouncing around in his head, trying to stay one step ahead of this conversation. He shouldn't bother, he'd never guess the ending.

Maybe getting it all out in one go was the best plan.

I lifted my chin. "The hunter I found under my porch. The one I healed. He's my...mate."

Baker spat out his drink. "What the fuck?"

For the second time this week, someone's drink sprayed all over my face. I wiped it off with the sleeve of my shirt.

Saying it out loud sent a weird zip through my blood as though I'd claimed him as mine, even though we hadn't sealed the bond.

Would we seal the bond?

Would my father accept him?

"Are you...sure?"

I hadn't had a lot of boyfriends growing up, not many guys would dare date the alpha's daughter, protected by all her beefy male cousins. I thought having no siblings would make my love life easier, but Baker and his brothers made up for my lack of older brothers.

The more I thought about it, the surer I was. I liked the way Wyatt made me feel, the way he looked at me as though I were a complex puzzle he wanted to spend eternity deciphering. I liked how my blood heated when he touched me, and how my heart squeezed when one side of his mouth kicked up in a sexy smirk. And don't even start me on those damn dimples.

"I'm positive." A smile lifted my cheeks. "It's not unheard of. Look at Noah, his mate is a witch."

"Witch. Not a hunter."

A lump thickened in my throat. Sure, Mia was a witch, not a hunter, but Wyatt was once a witch, too. Surely, everyone would see that.

"Layla."

I stilled when Wyatt said my name at the top of the stairs. How much had he heard? I almost slapped myself. Everything. I hadn't whispered, and with his heightened hearing, he would've heard every word. I should've told him first, but there wasn't an opportunity.

A low growl rumbled from Baker, his voice dark and deadly. "You should be dead."

Wyatt

I descended the stairs, glaring at the asshole shifter who'd left me for dead. His claw marks had almost killed me. If I hadn't made it to Layla's cabin...

Seeing him again stoked a red-hot rage through my blood. Magic and power bubbled inside me, threatening to unleash. My fingers curled into fists. I wanted to squeeze the air from his lungs, make him pay for what he'd done. Make him feel the pain he'd inflicted on me.

Glass shattered. I leaped over the handrail and charged at him, slamming him into the wall. Red dotted in my vision. His hands squeezed around my neck, choking me. I bared my fangs. Rage bubbled so close to the surface I struggled to rein in my hunter side. Even with the recent blood, it fought for control.

Layla squealed, pulling the guy's wrist. "Baker, stop. Don't."

Her voice broke through the haze. I tried to shove away from the shifter. The dude tightened his grip around my throat. Layla threw a punch at him, but he caught her fist with one hand just before it collided with his face.

"Let. Him. Go."

She stood toe to toe with the guy, her wild, vibrant eyes staring him down as though she were a foot taller. My chest would swell with pride if I could inhale.

Right before I thought I'd pass out, he shoved me backward. I stumbled and leaned over at the waist, sucking in gulps of air.

"This is the hunter you saved? He fucking attacked

our pack. Attacked *me*."

"And it seems you also attacked him." Layla acted so delicate on the outside but inside was the heart of a warrior. "Yes, this is the hunter. *My* hunter."

I straightened, moving closer to her, keeping a sharp eye on the shifter, Baker. After a long moment, the guy growled, and turned away.

Controlling the cravings was easier now that I'd had blood, but I sensed this guy would push my buttons. I needed to keep my hunter side in check around him. If I lost my shit again, I might just tear the guy's throat out.

Baker shoved a hand through his hair. "Fuck, Layla."

I stepped forward. "Watch your mouth."

He sneered at me. "You're lucky I don't shift right now and finish what I started."

"You don't scare me."

He stepped closer, inflating his chest. "I should. You're in a fucking town full of wolves."

Layla pushed Baker's shoulder. "Stop it." She pinned me with a furious glare. "Both of you."

Baker narrowed his eyes at me before looking away. I ran my tongue under the tip of a fang to stop from shoving the asshole in the back.

"Right. Now that we've got that awkward introduction out of the way, I need a drink too."

Layla poured herself a drink, but the shifter couldn't keep his damn mouth shut.

"We've gotten ourselves into some shit over the years, Lay, but this?" He pointed at me like I was some rodent rummaging through her trash.

"I couldn't let him die, Baker." She looked at me.

"He's my mate."

My heart beat all weird. Mate. I glanced at Layla. Was that why I felt an ancient tug when I thought of her? Why I couldn't leave even though I knew I should. Was that the strange sense of familiarity I experienced as though I'd loved her in a past life?

When she'd offered me her wrist, trusted me to take her blood when I struggled to control the hunger, something had shifted inside me. Even before that when I licked her finger. Tasting that first drop, awoke a fire in my soul. I felt...connected to her. I wasn't sure about mates, but I'd heard the stories. What I thought were myths.

"He saved me tonight." She gravitated to my side, and I ached to wrap my arms around her waist. "When the other hunter attacked, Wyatt pushed me out of the way."

"What if they're all working together?"

Sourness seeped down my throat. That wasn't too far from the truth. I'd initially come to Timber Falls hunting alpha blood, seizing the opportunity to blend in with a mass attack. They'd had the same objective. Instead, I'd found her, something much more precious. Was it fate? Was I meant to find her?

"Wyatt said there's a traitor in the pack."

Baker swore, his hand once again raking through his unruly hair. "Of course, he'd say that."

"It's true." Baker glared at me. I doubt we'd ever be besties, but I didn't care. "One of your wolves is working with hunters to take down the alpha."

chapter seventeen

Layla

I stared at the slight frown on Wyatt's face, and how his eyes remained deep gold rather than thin bright, amber slits. Everything about him seemed familiar, yet his words bounced around in my head making no sense.

Take down the alpha?

My father?

"What did you say?" Baker reacted first.

Wyatt's brows creased even more as he studied me before answering. "One of your pack is working with hunters."

My stomach twisted into tight knots. A traitor in the pack, who'd gone behind my father's back with the intention of...killing him. The idea made me sick. Who would do that? And why?

Finally, I found my voice. "What does he look like?"

Wyatt's jaw clenched as though he ground his molars. "I recognized the voice but didn't piece it together until I saw him in the forest tonight." His lip curled. "The douchebag who keeps fucking showing up at your door."

I gasped. "Trey?"

Baker swore under his breath. "I knew there was something off about him."

"We've known each other for years. I can't believe he'd...why would he...?"

My brain felt ready to explode. Trey. A traitor? Why would he want to kill my father? My father took him in, gave him sanctuary in our pack when he had nothing. He respected my father. Betraying him didn't make sense.

"Tell us what you know," Baker demanded.

Wyatt perched on the armrest of the couch, still giving me that curious look. Had he sensed the hitch in my heart rate? What would he do when he found out the alpha Trey targeted was my father?

"The dropkick met hunters outside town three nights before the attack. I wasn't traveling with them, just... happened to be in the right place at the right time."

"That's debatable," Baker grumbled, and I glared at him.

"He wants to take down the alpha. Why, I have no idea. But for a group of hunters, it's a win-win."

"What do you want to do?" Baker asked me.

I stared at the exposed beams in the ceiling again, hoping this time they'd give me direction. Which, of course, they didn't. They never did. I should call my father, let him know what happened tonight and about Trey. But something still didn't add up. Until I had proof, I couldn't accuse Trey of being a traitor, not based solely off Wyatt's word. Though, Wyatt had no reason to lie about it. And now I thought about it, the attack had been well orchestrated.

"Why would Trey admit to miscounting, and tell everyone there was a hunter still out there if he was working with them?"

Wyatt shifted slightly. "He wants me dead. His plan to take down the alpha failed, and I can identify him. He probably wants the whole pack to hunt me down and take care of his loose thread."

Baker swore again. "And it would've worked if another hunter hadn't shown up."

My mind raced. With my father out of town for the night, he was safe. That also gave us an opportunity to gather proof in case Trey planned another attack or came for Wyatt. He couldn't use the same excuse now that we'd taken down the remaining hunter. He'd have to be stealthier.

"Layla?" Wyatt's voice broke through my thoughts as his fingers curled around mine.

"You're not safe here." Realization smacked me in the head. "I think he knows you're here. I don't know how, but I think that's why he keeps showing up at my door."

Wyatt squeezed my hand. "That asshole is danger-ous. I don't give a fuck if he's after me, I won't leave you."

I snorted. Everyone around me was dangerous.

A floorboard creaked on the front porch. I froze. Baker's gaze darted to me as he held a finger over his lips. Wyatt stood, not making a sound. How was he so quiet? He pointed to the front window. Someone was out there.

"Get her out of here," Baker whispered.

"No," I snapped, just as quiet. "This is my home. If

Trey or anyone else thinks they can barge in and destroy that, they can go to hell."

Baker closed in, lowering his voice even more. "He's your mate. I respect that, but if another pack member finds him here, they might not. Trusting fate to create a shifter mate is one thing, but...a hunter? I'm not sure they'll accept it. And if it's Trey?"

Baker's face tightened, his mouth forming a grim line.

He was right.

Wyatt squeezed my hand, and I sensed he struggled between protecting me and staying to fight. If Trey was outside, he wouldn't hesitate to kill Wyatt, and I doubted Wyatt would back down.

Especially now.

I had to hide with Wyatt until we figured this out.

Someone knocked on the door. "Layla?"

Trey.

Ice shivered down my spine, and I tugged Wyatt back when he prowled toward the door.

"My truck's out back. There's a sleeping bag and food in case we needed to patrol for longer." Baker fished the keys out of his pocket and handed them to me. "Go to the caves. I'll cover for you here and see what dirt I can dig up on Trey. I'll call you at first light."

I nodded, squeezing his hand as a silent thank you for always having my back. God knows I didn't deserve such a loving and protective family.

Trey knocked again on the door. "Layla? Are you okay?"

Baker narrowed his eyes at Wyatt. "You do anything

to hurt her, and I'll make bloodlust look like a princess party. Hear me?"

Wyatt squared his shoulders, toe to toe with Baker. "Don't ever doubt what I'd do to protect her."

Baker mumbled something as he turned toward the door.

As quietly as we could, Wyatt and I slipped out the back and dashed to Baker's truck.

Once inside, I started the engine and sped off into the darkness, relying on memory rather than visual clues through the narrow forest roads. Baker and I had explored the mountain caves all the time as kids, pretending there was a hidden world buried deep within them. A peaceful world without bloodshed. We'd never told anyone where we went, and they became our secret hideaway. Our escape from the outside world and pack responsibilities. Countless times, we'd lost daylight and spent the night out there, under a glittery blanket of stars.

That was back when the town was safer. When hunters weren't brave enough to attack pack lands. They were more opportunists back then rather than calculated predators.

On the drive, I lost myself in thought. Wyatt must've sensed my need for silence because we hardly spoke. Dark, gloomy shadows flew past as I concentrated on the road wondering how we'd make it through this.

Wyatt was my mate.

It was so clear. I'd felt drawn to him in a way I couldn't explain. When I'd found him under my porch, I felt compelled to heal him, to save him. As though I would no longer be whole if I let him die. Sure, I was a healer, but the urge was stronger than that. Almost like the force had come from deep within my soul. Then, when I'd been in the forest and the other hunter had attacked, Wyatt protected me. He'd been in full hunter mode, dangerous power rolling off him, but he hadn't targeted me. I'd felt completely safe. I knew without a doubt, he'd never hurt me.

My father always said the universe created mates who weren't equals, but ones who made us better versions of ourselves. He said my mother had made him a better man, a stronger shifter, and he wouldn't be the alpha he was today without having met her. She steered him through the darkest nights, guiding him back to the light each time he lost himself. But even though he believed in, and had experienced the mate bond first-hand, it didn't mean he'd accept Wyatt.

Wyatt was still a hunter.

Part of a group who'd attacked our pack.

Each time I felt like I had a clear path, something reminded me of all the obstacles stacked in our way.

"We're almost there," I said, turning onto a narrow dirt road, mostly concealed by thick undergrowth.

Wyatt sat up straighter as I steered the truck onto the road leading around the mountain. After a few more minutes, we stopped where it ended.

"We walk from here."

Wyatt grabbed my hand as I reached for the door handle. "Layla, wait."

I twisted to face him.

His chin dipped, eyes heavy and...sad. "I'm sorry."

"For what?"

His thumb stroked the back of my hand, soothing the worry bubbling under the surface. "You name it. For hiding under your porch, for dragging you into this mess." He lifted his gaze, searching my eyes in the filtered moonlight. "For losing control earlier."

I couldn't help it. My thoughts rushed back to the moment I'd returned home to find him overtaken with bloodlust. He'd warned me, told me he wasn't in control, and still I hadn't left. I'd trusted him not to harm me. And when his fangs had punctured my skin, drawing the first drop of blood, my body all but combusted. I'd never felt desire so powerful in all my life.

"You didn't lose control, you stopped when I asked. You didn't hurt me."

I felt my cheeks heat. His bite had done exactly the opposite. It had created an intense rush I still felt simmering in my body.

A shadow swirled through his eyes. "I almost... wanted to. The monster in me wanted to drain every drop of your blood. To drown in your taste forever. But your voice, it kept luring me back to the surface." He trailed his fingers along my jaw, down my neck. "I feel it. The connection between us. I can't help believing we met for a reason, that the universe guided me to you."

Wild thrills zipped through me. He leaned in, hovering at my lips. The last time we'd kissed had been one big lusty blur. I'd been so consumed with passion, the ecstasy of him taking my blood, that I'd barely had a chance to appreciate the taste of his lips. Our kiss had been frantic and needy. I wanted to taste him again, but this time slower, savoring the moment.

Shuffling closer, I met him halfway and pressed my mouth against his. Tentative at first, he lightly nipped my bottom lip until an overwhelming urge overtook all sensible thought. Wyatt's hand slipped from my jaw moving around the back of my neck, coaxing me closer. His tongue swept along my bottom lip, and I opened for him, surrendering to the sensations blooming in my blood. Not to mention the heat centering in my core. I wriggled even closer, sliding my hands up and over his shoulders, holding on and never wanting to let go.

As his fingers tangled in my hair, my brain turned to mush. He tasted of warm winter nights by the fire, of aged merlot, of stolen midnight kisses. For so long, I'd craved peace between our kinds, to live in harmony with one another. A dream I thought until now, was impossible. Had the universe, fate, led Wyatt to me?

My mate bond had fired to life the moment I first saw him, I just hadn't recognized it.

Wyatt cradled my jaw in his strong hands, angling my head to deepen our kiss, his fingers continually stroking, touching as though he were afraid to let go. I sank into his embrace, forgetting all the obstacles between us, all the reasons why this was wrong, why the pack might reject our pairing.

I couldn't think about all that right now. I wanted to be in the moment, right here with Wyatt while we had the time. Tomorrow, when my father returned home, we'd face those obstacles head on. Together. Until then, every hard decision could wait.

Wyatt's thumbs swept along my jaw as he slowed our kiss, easing back to rest his forehead on mine. Our heavy breaths collided in the tiny space between our mouths. We stayed like that for the longest moment, breathing in each other's air, content. Happy.

Drawing back, I braced myself in case his eyes flashed amber, but they remained alluring gold. I tunneled my fingers through his thick, black hair. "We should get to the cave."

He leaned in and kissed me again, softer this time, a closed mouth kiss, lingering at my lips. His hands cradled my face making my heart heavy and light at the same time. I never wanted this to end.

chapter eighteen

Wyatt

Exiting the truck, I grabbed the sleeping bag, blankets, and lantern, while Layla slung a back-pack of supplies over her shoulder. Hand in hand, she led me along a narrow trail to the cave's entrance. Guided by the lantern, we found our way through the twisted tunnels before we arrived at a hidden chamber about the size of her living room. The air was cooler, thinner as though we were deep inside the mountain's belly.

I placed the lantern on the firm dirt and spread out the sleeping bag and a blanket, coaxing her down beside me.

Layla sat cross-legged, digging through the bag. "Let's see what Baker stashed in here. Probably nothing but chocolate and protein bars."

She rattled off a list, but I couldn't stomach food, not so soon after digesting blood.

A shiver shook her shoulders, and I draped the spare

blanket around her, pulling her closer. "Come here, I won't bite."

Mischief glinted in her eyes. "That's not entirely true."

I barked a laugh. "I won't bite unless you want me to. Is that better?"

The sharp intake of her breath made my pulse speed up. Had she enjoyed my bite? Taking blood from her was risky, but for some reason, it had felt right. As though her blood had unique properties, calling to me, fueling my power. Sure, shifter blood amplified a hunter's strength and extended their life span, but hers provided more. It didn't just strengthen me, it transformed the power surging through me into something I couldn't explain. Harnessing my magic came easier than ever before.

She'd given her trust so freely, and it created a strange mixture of emotions inside me.

Backpack forgotten, Layla leaned her head on my shoulder and snuggled closer. Calmness washed through me just as it had earlier in the night.

"Do you believe in fated mates?" she murmured.

I tossed the concept around in my head while I thought of an answer. "Honestly, I'm not sure what I believe any more."

So much had happened, so much cruelty, shitty life choices, and pain had led me on a destructive path with no end in sight. Did the universe lead me to Timber Falls to find Layla? At first, I thought meeting her was my path to curing the bloodlust. Then, the more time I spent with her, I figured she was my punishment for not saving Ellie. For failing to protect my family.

At this point in my life, failures outweighed accomplishments. Maybe fate sent me to Layla so she could heal my soul, make me fall for her, only to have that douchebag kill me.

Deliver hope, then crush it. That seemed more like it.

But that wasn't true. When I searched deep inside, right down beyond the layers of hurt and self-loathing, a single flame flickered in the darkness.

I rested my chin atop her head. "My ancestors spoke of destiny, of the push and pull of the universe. How every action caused a reaction. How every death gives life and vice versa. Balance." I wrapped an arm around her shoulders, needing her closer. "I feel like you're my balance."

Her arm curled around my stomach, playing with the side hem of my shirt. "I feel the same. Being here with you feels...right."

I exhaled a shaky breath. I couldn't deny it, I felt it, too. I'd met Layla for a reason, I just wasn't sure why.

Toying with her hair, I twisted a stray strand around my finger. Now that the chaos of my life had quieted, it felt as though my world had finally settled. The sane part of me, regardless of how minute that was, whispered we were destined. But how could that be true? Our worlds were so different.

Drinking her blood and controlling my thirst defied the stories handed down from generation to generation. Shifters and hunters were ancient enemies, not lovers. Yet, despite all that stood against us, our connection held me here with her.

I didn't know how it happened, but something inside

me transformed. No, not transformed, awoke. As though Layla had unlocked a secret door, leading to an existence I never imagined. A beacon of hope soared through my blood until I saw nothing but the beautiful, fierce, determined woman before me.

She saw my flaws, my demons, and still refused to turn away.

Capturing her face in my hands, I kissed her with everything I had. All the power left in my soul, my fears, my hopes for a brighter future. With her in my arms, the world didn't seem so angry, so cold, so bleak. She was the fiery light at the end of my dark and lonely existence.

Layla

Kissing Wyatt made me forget the outside world existed. I forgot about Trey and how he betrayed my pack. Instead, as Wyatt's tongue swept over mine, I effortlessly envisioned a world where we weren't so different. One where he wasn't a hunter, a descendent from an ancient coven of witches who'd centuries ago, battled my kind for territory and power, turning themselves into bloodthirsty killers. I also pretended I wasn't a shifter, the same kind who'd murdered his family.

I imagined peace.

Before long, he drew back to lay down, resting my head on his chest. My heart beat strong and steady as Wyatt's dark, mysterious scent coupled with the damp moss from the cave, calmed me even more.

Regardless of our differences, how we fought on opposite sides of the war, we were destined.

Slowly, I turned my head. Wyatt peered down at me in the crook of his arm and all my hopes for a different future, one where we could be together, reflected in his eyes.

My entire life, my father had spoken of the mate bond, and how each shifter sensed it in a different way. I sensed it now. But when it came to my pack, my responsibilities, would sensing a mate bond be enough to convince them Wyatt wasn't the enemy?

This man, the one who entwined his destiny with mine without even knowing.

He brushed the back of his knuckles along my jaw as I lost myself in his lingering gaze. Even if my father refused to support our bond, I could never mate with someone else. I could never accept anything less than what I felt in my heart right now.

In my soul.

I wanted to tie myself to him for the rest of my life.

A slow smile crept on Wyatt's face as he lifted his hand and waved it across the cave ceiling, producing a smattering of sparkly stars. With the next wave, lights burst across the space. A mesmerizing display of vibrant colors flickering in the darkness as though we were outside beneath the night sky watching brilliant fireworks. Millions and millions of them.

Each time he waved his hand back and forth in the air between us and the ceiling more colors exploded in the darkness.

"Your magic," I whispered.

His arm curled around me, drawing me closer as he placed a gentle kiss on my forehead. My heart ached, yet at the same time felt so full, ready to burst.

So complete.

"I'm not naïve," he murmured, still swaying his hand back and forth. "I know our two kinds aren't meant to be together. But if I've learned anything over the decades, it's how life is about living. Taking each moment in both hands and truly living the best life you can. Not letting fear hold you back."

He lowered his arm to tangle his fingers with mine as we both watched the stars explode above us.

"I lost sight of that along the way. I've wasted so many years seeking revenge, to avenge my sister." He shifted slightly to turn his head to me. "When all along, I should've been searching for you."

My soul burst into millions of glittery stars and floated up to join the others.

"If things were different, I'd whisk you away. We'd travel the world, experience all its wonder. Nothing would matter, only that we were together."

I lifted onto my forearm. The exploding stars reflected in his eyes and in that moment, it didn't matter whether he was a hunter, or that I was a shifter. In the cave, tangled in each other's arms, we were simply Wyatt and Layla. Two lost souls who'd finally found each other.

"We don't know what the future holds, all we have is now. We have this moment. Tonight." I placed my palm on his chest, over the steady thump of his heart. "I want to take this moment with both hands and live it."

His hand traveled along my waist to settle on my hip. "I want you, Layla. More than I've ever wanted anything in this world. But I know what being with me does. You can't tie yourself to a hunter. You deserve better, a mate who is your kind, one who is worthy of your love." His thumb idly circled my hip sending tiny shivers through my middle. "Not a monster."

Oh, God. My heart couldn't take any more.

"You're not a monster, Wyatt." I traced his jaw with the back of my fingers. "One day, there could be peace between our kinds. We don't have all the answers. We only have now."

As he searched my eyes, I witnessed something other than need or bloodlust. I saw yearning as though he too craved acceptance, peace. Me.

I brushed my thumb along his bottom lip. "I want this with you. I want us. I want to savor this moment and remember it forever."

The scorching heat of his hand slipped beneath the hem of my shirt and splayed over my lower back. "If we do this, it'll be forever."

I nodded.

"Are you sure that's what you want?"

My heart accelerated, not because of nerves, but anticipation. "I'll never feel like this with anyone else. My family believes that the universe creates mates who strengthen us, who make us strive to be better. No other guy could make me feel the strength you do. No one else could make me feel this...whole. Regardless of what happens in our future, for me, it will only ever be you."

Indecision bounced in his eyes as he peered into mine. "Layla."

"I want this, Wyatt. I want you."

chapter nineteen

Layla

While the magical stars continued to reflect colors over the cave walls, Wyatt curled his hand around my nape and drew my mouth to his. He kissed me heartbreakingly slowly as I melted into his embrace. Without breaking our kiss, he rolled me onto my back and hovered over me, cupping my jaw.

His tongue swept over my bottom lip, and I opened for him, giving him my all.

My heart, my body, my soul.

He kissed me so gently, I thought I would shatter. I'd die right there on the ground.

I didn't worry about what would happen later, tomorrow, next week or years from now. I didn't concern myself with the barriers between our two worlds or if his blood-lust would rear its head while I kissed him. I surrendered to our joined mouths, allowing the sensations to float me up to those glittery stars.

And I never wanted to come back down.

Breathless, Wyatt trailed his lips down my neck,

along my collar bone, worshipping my skin as though I were a goddess. I'd never experienced such pleasure. A feeling of...rightness.

I'd never recover from this.

Wyatt eased back to sit on his haunches and pulled me upright in front of him. He cradled my face between his strong hands and took my mouth in a fierce, possessive kiss that shattered my heart.

I welcomed every sensation, every emotion, swelling inside me.

I tugged his shirt up and over his head, desperate to touch more of him. Determined to savor the moment, I trailed my fingers down his smooth chest, along the hard peaks of his muscles, over the faint scar in his side—the only reminder that a few days ago, he'd almost died.

Gently, he curled a finger beneath my chin, lifting my gaze. "For centuries, people have worshiped the sun. But for me, the moon creates the purest light. It shines, bravely chasing away the darkness, knowing each night it faces an endless battle. The darkness will return once the light descends, and the battle will begin again." He trailed his thumb over the fluttering pulse in my neck. "You are my moon, Layla. The shining light that lures me from the darkness, so I can face another day. You've given me life."

Tears burned in my eyes as I eased my mouth to his. He thought I pulled him from the darkness, but somehow, without knowing, I'd been wandering around there with him. I just hadn't been able to see.

Until now.

Wyatt lowered me onto my back and shifted between

my legs. He never took his gaze off me, not even when he slid down the zipper on my jeans and tugged them off my legs. The look in his eyes was pure sin. His lips trailed a hot path up the inside of my thighs. My entire body tingled, tiny tremors quaking through my limbs. Reaching the apex, his hot breath whispered against my panties, and I all but died.

"I want to touch you forever."

I tangled my fingers in his ragged hair. "That sounds like a brilliant idea."

Those dimples deepened as he gave me a wicked grin. He dragged his finger along the outside of my panties making me gasp. I already knew what his skilled fingers could do, how they'd brought me to the most powerful heights before plunging me into a pool of bliss. But this time felt different. He wasn't a shifter, yet the possession burning in his eyes, told me this time he'd claim me. He'd make me his. That he'd transport me beyond this world, and I'd never want to return.

And I was ready for it.

Lowering his mouth, he trailed kisses along my hip while he slipped his fingers in the waistband of my panties and slowly dragged them off. Cold air tingled my moistened skin, curling my toes.

His feather-light touch explored every inch of skin between my legs before arriving back at my center. My eyes rolled as a soft moan escaped me. Staring at the exploding stars, I surrendered to his touch. To the way his eyes promised so much more than pleasure, they stole my breath.

He stroked and circled the millions of nerves with his

finger while he kissed my belly, my hips, my thighs. His touch consumed me. Was this what it felt like to be with my mate?

I lost my train of thought when his tongue replaced his finger, licking me. I cried out. Waves of heat flashed through my middle, making my back arch off the ground. But Wyatt didn't relent. With one hand, he held me in place while he lapped and sucked, drawing gasp after gasp from me. He slipped a finger inside, careening me higher and higher to that magical cliff. My hands clutched the blanket beneath me, trying to keep my body on the ground and my mind, in the here and now. Above, those beautiful stars continued to burst and explode with light, so much my mind muddled from the overload of senses.

Wyatt moved his mouth to the crease between my hips and thighs. Something sharp scraped my skin but didn't puncture.

His fangs.

Instantly, memories of him drawing blood from my wrist burst in my mind, shattering me into a million pieces. I dove off that cliff headfirst, so hard and fast my vision blurred. Over and over, I shuddered while his fangs grazed my skin, his finger pumping inside me.

As the tremors lightened, Wyatt eased his finger out and hovered over me, his hands braced on either side of my head.

"I want this with you but..." The guttural need in his voice shivered through my middle. He swore, bowing his head. "I don't have protection. I wasn't planning..."

I cupped the side of his stubbly jaw. This beautiful,

broken man still thought of me, protected me. He could sink his fangs into my neck and drain my blood and in this moment, I wouldn't even blink.

My heart beat a little faster at the thought.

"I'm a modern woman, I have us covered with birth control. And I presume you can't get human diseases just like me?"

He nodded. "Thank fuck. Cause I really need to be inside you."

I needed that too, more than I cared to admit. The urge to claim him, seal our mate bond, consumed me. It thrummed in my blood, building in intensity as my wolf prowled inside me, demanding I take over control.

I wanted hours to explore his tall, muscular body, and trace all the grooves with my lips, but first I needed to claim him. To settle my wolf, ease the craving.

Wyatt scooted back only long enough to rip off his jeans before returning between my legs. He loomed over me, searching my eyes as unsaid words passed between us. Questions and hopes I couldn't think about. My only focus was being with him here and now.

Snaking my hand around his nape, I drew him down to my mouth. Slowly, at first, our kiss bled right to my soul, splitting it in half before melding it back together. Stronger. More whole than it was before. Warmth flared in my chest, and my wolf clawed, growing more impatient with the need to claim her mate.

I rocked along the outside of his hardness, aching for him.

"Wyatt..."

With his mouth still on mine, he reached between us

and positioned himself at my entrance. He drew back slightly and peered down at me with a look that told me he'd not only protect me, but he'd walk through the fires of hell for me. That he gave me not just his body, but his soul.

I cradled his jaw in my hands as he slid inside me, slowly filling me, stretching me. Those tiny glittery stars above our heads shattered along with my heart.

This man, my mate, broke me.

My hands curved over his broad shoulders as he trailed feverish kisses along my jaw, rocking inside me. I'd never recover from this. Never again would I experience sex with this much intensity.

If we only had this moment, I prayed it lasted forever.

His lips kissed, sucked, and nipped along my collar bone, down my neck, building me higher and higher. A sudden primal urge swept through me, stalling my breath. I didn't only want him inside me and to claim him. I wanted all of him, and I wanted him to have all of me.

Was it reckless?

Probably, but with him inside me, nothing had ever been clearer.

As his mouth trailed back up my neck, over my fluttering pulse, I angled my head, giving him more access. His body stilled.

He drew back, and I braced myself for the amber glow of his thin cat-like eyes, but it never happened.

"Layla..." His voice was thick and gravelly, his pointy fangs just visible below his top lip.

I ran my thumb over one and a shudder rippled through him. "I trust you."

I'd never been so sure of something in my entire life.

A low growl rumbled in his chest. "I don't need blood. The bloodlust is at bay."

"You don't need to take it, but I want to give it. I want to feel you drink from me while you're inside me. I want to give you all of me."

"Fuck."

His heated gaze dipped to my neck then back to me.

"Take from me, Wyatt."

Something in my eyes must've confirmed my words because he lowered his mouth and began to rock inside me once more. Delicious burns swept through me in time with his slow, deep thrusts, while his hot breath tingled my neck.

Sweet anticipation burned through me as he scraped his fangs on the sensitive flesh a second before he punctured my skin. I cried out. My entire body shuddered beneath him as he drew the first pull. Fire scorched through my blood, racing around my insides, quickly abating the sting of his bite. Coils of pleasure tightened in my center. He rocked faster, harder, drawing long, deep pulls of blood. My hands curled around his back, scoring his flesh, holding him against me.

Mine.

A single word flashed in my mind over and over. My mate.

Too soon, Wyatt released the seal from my neck with a lap of his tongue and drew back to peer into my eyes.

Everything I'd ever hoped for reflected in his gaze, and I finally saw it for what it was.

Love.

As my heart swelled, I captured his face in my hands and kissed him, soaring us both over the cliff into the blissful abyss.

chapter twenty

Wyatt

Layla snuggled in the crook of my arm, her long hair tumbling over my shoulder, warm body plastered against mine. I inhaled a deep breath of the intoxicating scent, committing it to memory. I never wanted this to end. If we lay naked in this cave for the rest of our lives, I'd die happy.

"That was..." I didn't have the words, let alone the brain power to describe how being with her had shattered everything inside me.

"Perfect," she whispered.

Not quite. I would've preferred to have taken her somewhere comfortable where I could've explored every inch of her body, every dip and groove, rather than in a damp cave while hiding from a traitor in her pack.

I didn't expect this between us. But now that I'd had her, I'd never get enough of the taste of her lips, how her eyes illuminated the darkness as she trembled beneath me. Or the soft moans that escaped her lips as I devoured her.

I twirled a strand of her platinum hair around my finger, tightening and loosening the hold. Although I'd love nothing more than to lay here with her in my arms ignoring the outside world, eventually this haven would end. I needed to end it. Finding that douchebag and finishing him became my priority before Layla was caught in the fight.

Soon.

Just not right now.

Before I ruined our peaceful bubble, I craved a few more moments of only me and her.

I drew her closer. She draped a leg over mine, and I tugged the blanket up over her shoulders.

"Do you make a habit of rescuing dangerous creatures and healing them?" I continued playing with her hair. The silky strands calmed me in a strange way.

She snorted, lifting onto her forearm so I could see her face. "Hardly. That was a one-time thing."

"Good." Her hair flopped in front of her face, and I tucked it behind her ear. I could touch it all day. "Just so you know, I'm not a fan of you rescuing other dudes and hiding them in your cabin."

The corner of her lips kicked up. "Is that so?"

I grunted in agreement. I didn't know what our future held, but I sure as shit didn't want her putting her life at risk for another asshole like me. The thought alone tightened a hot coil in my gut.

"So, what now?"

She returned her head to my shoulder, idly drawing circles on my bare chest. "My father will be back in the morning. I need to tell him about Trey and how he's working with hunters. And then..." Her chest inflated with a deep inhale. "And then I'll tell him about us. As alpha, if he supports our mate bond, the rest of the pack will too."

I choked on air. "Your father is the alpha of Timber Falls?"

She nodded. "Which is a good thing for us."

Fuck.

Bile rose in my throat. I'd fucking targeted her father for his blood so I could cure the curse and end this madness.

Her father.

A traitor in her pack paled in comparison to that shit.

Alpha blood was the missing ingredient. All I needed was a few drops so no other witch would go through what Ellie had. But now, the thought of betraying Layla, hurting her family, took a hammer to my chest.

If she ever found out why I'd come here, she'd never forgive me.

Any chance of a future with Layla died in a fiery explosion. Her father was the key to curing the curse, yet, for once, it wasn't what I craved. I'd spent so many years searching for a cure, following lead after lead, for it to grind to a halt when I fell in love with a shifter. The alpha's fucking daughter.

Layla tucked herself closer to me, but I no longer felt any warmth. Only coldness slowly freezing my veins.

"For so long, I've craved peace between our kinds. My father knows that. But he's seen more devastation than I can ever imagine. He won't take kindly to Trey's betrayal." She lifted her head and a hint of uncertainty lingered in her bright blue eyes. "But I worry more about what it means for us."

That chill turned to ice.

I tried to swallow the boulder in my throat. "What will he do if he finds out about us, sweetheart?"

Her lips rolled inward. "I'd like to believe our mate bond means more to him than what you are, but..." Her lashes lowered. "Part of me feels like I've also betrayed him."

She eased her head back down on my shoulder, and I tried to process the grenade she'd tossed in my lap.

Betrayal.

That word stoked something dark and feral inside me. I was a hunter with a skewed moral compass at best, having done unspeakable things to avenge my sister. But being the reason Layla betrayed her father, made me want to set the world on fire.

I wanted to protect her, to fight for her, to cure my bloodlust so she wouldn't have to choose between me and her family. But when curing my curse meant harming her father, and when being with her meant her betraying her family, I...couldn't. I'd rather be a monster for all eternity than ask that of her.

Family was everything.

Without it, life was a bleak and lonely existence.

If I were a wolf or an ordinary witch, maybe we could overcome the centuries of war. But a hunter. Her ancient enemy?

I'd given up my life because of the curse. I wouldn't make her do the same.

Turning my head away, I stared at the pitch-black ceiling, no longer smattered with bright stars.

Only one path was clear. Ensure her safety. Even if it meant forgoing the cure and instead, surrendering to my monster.

Layla

I woke and lay there for a moment with my eyes closed enjoying the lightness radiating in my chest. In a few short weeks, no, days, Wyatt had changed my life. I'd saved a guy who'd given me more hope for peace than I'd ever had. At times, I'd fought a losing battle not only with my father, but all shifters. But Wyatt proved not all hunters were monsters. They had feelings, hopes and dreams, just like everyone else.

Now, no one craved peace more than me.

Wyatt and I could change the war. End it even. Together we could accomplish more than I'd ever dreamed. We could usher in a new era. I prayed Father wouldn't overreact and kill Wyatt before I finished speaking.

I'd found my mate, something not every shifter did. Some shifters searched their entire lives for the other half of their soul, only to never find them. They became a lone wolf or simply took a lover for companionship, but the mate bond, that feeling of completeness was forever absent.

I was lucky. Though now, having experienced the bond, I could never love another. Wyatt was it for me. If he needed time to adjust, I'd respect that. Because eventually, I believed we'd find a way through this.

Stretching my legs, I rolled over and reached for Wyatt, only to pat an empty space beside me. Cool air rushed beneath the blankets pooled at my waist as I sat up and switched on the lantern. "Wyatt?"

He wasn't here. His clothes, his jacket, his shoes. Him. Gone.

"Wyatt?" I called louder.

I thought back to our conversation during the early hours of this morning before exhaustion lulled me to sleep. How he murmured a vow to always protect me, no matter the cost.

Heaviness sank on my chest.

Did he have second thoughts? When I'd confessed my fears about my father not accepting us, his demeanor shifted. Had I sabotaged our relationship before it truly began? Did he leave so I wouldn't have to choose between him and my pack? I was fairly certain that wouldn't happen, but was that what he meant by protecting me?

Why didn't he just tell me how he felt? Why didn't he wake me?

With Wyatt out there somewhere, it was now even more crucial I told my father everything—from the moment I found Wyatt injured under my porch until now. Minus the, uh, blood sharing and sex because no father wanted those details about his only daughter. Then, I'd find Wyatt.

The important part was not all hunters were blood-thirsty killers. Not all hunters targeted shifters for the sake of it.

I'd experienced the other side of this war, and it only made me more determined for peace.

Gathering my things, I rolled up the sleeping bag and stuffed everything back into Baker's backpack. A strange sensation quivered through my chest, settling like lead in my belly. I stilled, concentrating, trying to identify the source. Something felt wrong, but I couldn't quite figure out what. When the feeling eased, I slung the backpack over my shoulder.

At the entrance to the cave, I paused and peered back into the darkness, remembering the brilliant exploding stars Wyatt had created with a sweep of his hand. My chest ached. I'd felt his love last night, in his gentle touch, his lingering glances, in the way he...

My fingers brushed the sensitive spot on my neck where his fangs had punctured.

He'd claimed me as I'd claimed him.

The sensation in the pit of my stomach returned. Urgency. This time, I couldn't brush it off. I turned and bolted through the tunnels, exiting to the early-morning light. My phone pinged with an incoming message. Followed by another. Six missed calls and twelve text messages, all from Baker. The last message sent a shiver down my spine.

Baker: *Code fucking red.*

I fumbled with my phone, holding it up to my ear as I raced to the truck. Baker answered on the first ring.

"Thank fuck."

"What the hell's going on?" I asked, throwing the backpack in the bed of the truck.

"He captured him, Lay. Trey has your mate."

chapter twenty-one

Layla

I punched my foot on the gas, pushing Baker's truck as fast as it would go. Trey had captured Wyatt. My mate. How in the hell had that happened?

A sudden urge to rip heads from bodies consumed me as my hands tightened around the steering wheel. If I needed more evidence that Wyatt was my mate, this was it. I'd resort to bloody murder to get him back.

Hunters weren't so different from us after all.

I swerved around a bend in the road, tires screeching. Trey had better prepare because what I'd do to make sure Wyatt was safe would make a hunter look like a cute kitten.

A flicker of white flashed in my peripheral as a snow-white wolf caught up with the truck, sprinting alongside.

Baker.

I slammed on the brakes. In one swift movement, Baker shifted back to human form and darted to the truck. He grabbed a spare set of clothes from the bed and shoved them on. My hands shook so badly I struggled to unlock the damn door.

Baker rapped his knuckles on the driver's side window. "Let me drive."

I didn't argue. I scooted over to the passenger seat. The second I buckled my belt, Baker took off down the road. Trees flew by in a blur, and I looked away before I puked.

I pressed the heel of my hand against my chest, attempting to quell the sharp pain. "How did this happen? How did they find him? He was with me."

Until he left.

"Fucking Trey, that's how. He was cagey last night when I said you weren't there. He would've heard the truck leave."

I sucked in a sharp breath. "He must've followed us."

Too many unanswered questions left my brain feeling like it would explode over the windshield.

My stomach whirled. "Is he...alive?"

Through our mate bond, I sensed he was, but the connection was so...faint.

Baker's hand curled around the steering wheel, turning his knuckles white. Each second he didn't answer sharpened the pain in my chest until inhaling felt like it would slice open my lungs.

Finally, Baker glanced to me. "I'm not going to lie, Lay. He's barely hanging on."

A strangled cry escaped my lips.

My voice rose. "My father issued a blanket kill-on-sight for any hunters. What if Trey..." I gasped and swiveled to Baker. "He knows. Trey must know Wyatt's my mate. He'd be able to scent the bond."

Baker grabbed my hand and squeezed it tight. "We'll save him, Lay."

I refused to let the tears slide down my cheeks. I was stronger than that. I wouldn't give up, not yet. Not ever. I'd never been one to concede, and I sure as hell wouldn't start now. I wouldn't sit in this truck and let a traitor kill my mate.

I'd kick down the door and save him.

Anger bubbled under the surface, swallowing the sadness as my wolf clawed to shift. To save our mate. I sent a silent promise that when the time came, we'd do whatever it took to save him. Anything. Even if that involved taking down a pack member.

Impatience coiled my muscles as adrenaline fired through my veins, it took everything in me not to shift right there in the truck.

"He's in the cells?" I glared at Baker as he turned onto a familiar track. "Trey has my mate in a goddamn cell?"

Baker didn't answer, he didn't need to. I knew this area of the forest, at the far end of my father's property. He didn't use it like our ancestors had during the less humane times in our history. Back then, shifters would capture hunters and torture them. Sometimes even witches.

Now, we just killed them.

Was that any better?

"Is my father back yet?"

"No. He can't reach town. Flooding cut off the road

to Timber Falls." Baker slowed the truck to a crawl. "Trey wouldn't try something this stupid if Rhett were here."

I thought of calling him, but what good would that do? He'd probably shift and race back to town, putting more of us in danger.

Baker stopped the truck when he approached the clearing. I reached for the door, but he grabbed my arm.

"Be smart, Lay. If Trey's still there, you can't just barge in and demand he release your mate."

"Damn right I can."

"Think about it. If Trey really is a traitor who coordinated a hunter attack on the pack, on *your* pack, why would he keep one alive? Why would he capture Wyatt and hold him in the cells?"

A shiver trickled down my spine. Baker was right. Trey did this for a reason, and I needed to figure out his agenda. Now wasn't the time to blindly barge in and demand things. If I didn't play this right, someone would end up dead. I needed to think like an alpha. How would my father handle it? If someone from our pack had held my mother captive, what would my father have done?

Burned the place down.

Only, my mother wasn't a hunter, she wasn't even a witch. Regardless, my father would've stopped at nothing to make sure she was safe. Even if Wyatt had intended to leave, even if I'd scared him off with my talk of the future, I wouldn't stand by and let him die. I'd fight for him. For us.

I threw open the door and peered back at Baker. "You have my back?"

His intense gaze never wavered. "Always."

If I had more time, I'd take a moment to appreciate the warmth swelling in my chest. Baker wasn't only my cousin, he was my best friend. And one day, when my father stepped down and I became alpha of Timber Falls, he'd make a kickass second. There was no one else I trusted more.

Unlike Trey.

"Let's do this."

I didn't run, nor did I creep through the forest trying to sneak up on Trey. I held my chin high, shoulders straight, with my stride deliberate and purposeful. Baker remained close behind me every step.

I slowed as we approached the decrepit stone structure carved into the foot of the mountain. Trey stood by the ancient, grated door, leaning on the wall as though he hadn't a care in the world. No remorse. No guilt. I had the biggest urge to smash him in the face. Then, shift and let my wolf tear apart his flesh.

What was wrong with me? Violence was never the answer...until now.

"Where is he?" I demanded.

Trey tilted his head. "You should thank me. I'm saving you from making a mistake that could result in your exile."

Inside, my wolf growled, snapping her jaws to have a piece of this traitor. "I said, where is he?"

"Does your father know you fucked a hunter?"

Hot and wild rage erupted inside me. I roared, launching at Trey but strong arms wrapped around my middle, holding me back.

"Aww, Baker, your loyal watchdog saves the day."

Baker growled by my ear. "Watch it, asshole."

"If you've hurt him, I'll kill you."

Trey barked a laugh and pushed off the wall. "Sooner or later, you'll see I did this for you, Layla."

I stilled as Baker's earlier warning repeated in my head. I needed to play this smart. If I didn't, if I slipped up, one of us wouldn't make it out alive.

I shoved from Baker's grasp and stood toe to toe with Trey. "What do you want?"

His gaze softened, reminding me of the boy my father had found orphaned. A lone wolf. The same boy who'd given me handpicked daisies when we'd sat outside, too young to attend pack meetings.

"All I want is what's best for you. I'm protecting you, Layla." His gaze darted over my shoulder to Baker. "Unlike you. That's your entire job and you failed."

Fury bubbled under my skin, and I'd never wanted to inflict pain more than I did now. I was meant to heal shifters, not injure them. "How is kidnapping my mate protecting me?"

Trey's brows knitted as though I should already know the answer. "Do you know why your so-called mate came to Timber Falls? The real reason, not whatever tale he spun you."

A knot coiled in my belly. Wyatt had said he'd stumbled on the other hunters, that he'd come here for...my face tingled. He hadn't told me why. I knew he sought revenge for his sister. But he'd never told me why he'd chosen to attack this town.

When I didn't answer, a smug smirk lifted at the corner of Trey's mouth. "Your father. The hunter stayed with you to get close to your father. It was all part of his ploy. He preyed on your goodwill, Layla."

"What?"

Trey flashed a perfect smile with perfect white teeth I wanted to smash.

I snatched the front of his shirt so fast, twisting it in my fist. "Answer me."

"He knew you'd heal him. He allowed Baker to injure him just enough then hid where only you'd find him."

"That's bullshit. I fought him. He wasn't pretending," Baker said from behind me.

Trey cocked a brow. "And yet, he lived."

Chills racked my blood as I staggered back.

No. Surely, Wyatt hadn't staged our meet. He hadn't used me.

"He knew you wouldn't tell the pack. He knew the alpha's daughter wouldn't risk blabbing to her father about saving a hunter." Trey leaned in so close I'd head-butt him if I weren't so stunned. "And then after you healed him, he seduced you."

"Fuck off, asshole," Baker snapped. "Layla, don't listen to this shit. You can't fake the mate bond."

Trey straightened. "He used you to get close to your father. All he wants is alpha blood to cure the bloodlust. Don't shoulder all the blame. He probably used a witch concoction to make you fall for him. Those original families are powerful even as hunters."

I couldn't speak. Couldn't think clearly.

What I'd felt for Wyatt last night when we'd sealed the bond...how he'd touched me...how the need to give myself to him had consumed every part of my soul. Wyatt couldn't fake it, and there wasn't a spell that could make me feel as strongly for him as I did.

That I knew of.

"You're lying."

"You're going to trust the word of a bloodthirsty hunter, an enemy to our pack, someone who used you, over one of your own?"

Doubt was a slippery, dark shadow seeping into my mind. My father had taken Trey in as a young teen, raised him, eventually granting him a position of power within the pack. Sure, I'd known him for years, but did that override my feelings for Wyatt?

Were those feelings even real?

"I'm on your side, Layla. Once Rhett finds out how... compromised you are, he'll never let you become alpha. You'll be an embarrassment to the pack. He'll probably hand over alpha to one of Baker's stupid older brothers, and all the sacrifices I've made will be for nothing."

I frowned at his strange choice of words.

"What sacrifices?"

I caught the slight twitch at the corner of his eyes.

Trey softened his voice as though speaking only to me. "Take me as your mate, and I'll make this problem of yours disappear."

"Are you for real? Why would I...?" My stomach sank as all the pieces clicked together. "You want to lead the pack."

"Do this and your father will never need to know about your indiscretion."

"Are you...blackmailing me? You orchestrated an

attack to kill him." My voice rose. "What about all the shifters who died that night? Do you even care?"

"If the reward is great enough, Layla, there'll always be collateral damage."

I seethed. "I'd never mate with you. Never. Not before, and especially not now."

He curled his lip and rage like I'd never seen darkened his eyes. "That's because you have a thing for bloodsuckers."

Everything happened in a blur. Baker roared, launching past me. A sickening crunch made me wince. Numbness clawed into my blood, spreading from my toes all the way to my face until I stood there in the middle of the forest, frozen. Over to the side, Baker and Trey fought in wolf form. Vicious snarls and snapping jaws faded away as blood whooshed in my ears. My gaze lifted to the metal door at the entrance to the cells.

Had Wyatt lied to me? Had he used me to get close to my father?

I thought destiny brought Wyatt to my cabin, that I was meant to find him and heal him. When he'd only ever been interested in a cure. Realization swayed my vision. Wyatt left me this morning, he had no intention of staying, of building a future with me. He only ever wanted my father's—

"Oh, God."

My hand flung to my throat. I gave him my blood. I gave Wyatt my blood. Not the alpha blood he'd hoped for, but blood all the same. I'd healed a hunter who targeted my father.

I heaved as the bile rose in my throat.

Slowly, my vision sharpened on the door. A strange sense of calm washed over me as I took one step toward it, then another. I had to know. I had to know the truth, to look Wyatt in the eyes and hear him admit it.

I forced my feet to keep moving as I heaved open the door and descended the stone steps, lit by torches hung on the damp walls. I'd come here once as a kid and never returned. The place smelled of...death. Heaviness laced the air with the weight of all the tortured souls.

My stomach churned, but I swallowed the nausea.

I was here for one thing: the truth.

A pack member stood guard at the cell door. Deakin. He'd been in the forest on patrol with us the other night when the second hunter attacked. Given his wide eyes, he clearly didn't expect me to make it this far.

I jutted my chin, fueling my voice with dormant alpha power. "Move."

Deakin's hand slipped to the knife strapped to his thigh.

"Touch that blade, and I'll claw you to pieces."

The guy held my stare for a second before he found some common sense and bowed his head. He stepped aside and my heart tore into two. Wyatt was on his knees, his arms stretched behind him, held in place by black manacles secured to the wall. Blood dripped from cuts over his body, pooling on the dirt.

My fingers curled around the iron bar as Wyatt lifted his head.

chapter twenty-two

Wyatt

A soft whisper of midnight roses roused my consciousness. The air felt lighter, cleaner, more heavenly. I inhaled a deep—

A sharp pain shot through my chest stealing any air I managed to inhale. Probably the result of broken ribs.

Chains rustled before a metal grate slid open. I strained, forcing one eye to open. One was so swollen it refused to, the throbbing extending right to the back of my head.

A blurry figure walked toward me, throwing my mind back to the moment I first saw her.

My angel.

"Lay..." My voice sounded all wrong. Groggy. Hoarse.

I blinked a few times, trying to focus on her. She held back, a few steps away from me, her arms by her sides.

"Is it true?" Her voice hitched.

I wracked my brain struggling to remember what had happened. I'd left a cave to hunt down the traitor. To end the threat to her pack. But the shot had come out of nowhere. A sharp sting at the back of my neck.

"Layla," I winced, my tongue too thick for my mouth. "Traitor."

"The shifter you call a traitor told me why you came to Timber Falls."

I lifted my head too fast. My vision went haywire. That asshole had kicked me in the head more times than I could count and whatever was in that shot neutralized my powers.

Layla stepped forward, glaring down at me. "Why did you attack Timber Falls?"

Despite her warrior's heart, I was conscious enough to hear her voice crack. The pain in my ribs drifted to the center of my chest.

The more I focused on her features, the more my vision cleared. Her eyes darkened. Flickering light from a lantern hung outside the cell, reflected across her face. A face I'd kissed, touched, loved.

I swallowed, wincing as it burned down my throat.

I'd come to Timber Falls for her father's blood and at the time, I hadn't cared how I accessed it. But everything had changed once I met her.

"Did you use me to get to my father?"

My reply jammed in my throat, but somehow, Layla sensed it.

She recoiled. "It's true."

"Layla." I reached for her only to have the chains binding my wrist cut into the flesh. "When I found out you knew about the local pack, I thought I could use that information. But that was before...I knew what you were. Who you are." I swallowed again. "What you are to me."

The fire in her glare burned along my exposed skin. "And when you found out I was a wolf, you thought that was even better? That I could lead you right to the alpha." Her voice rose. "That you could kill my father for a cure that doesn't even exist."

My shoulders sagged, held up only by the chains.

"It does. Ellie found it in the grimoire before she..." I lifted my head and the tears in Layla's eyes undid me. "I was so desperate to end the bloodlust. To end the suffering. Yes, I stayed in the beginning because you could lead me to the pack, but then everything changed. In the end, Layla, I stayed for you. Not for a cure, not to get close to your father. I stayed for you."

Silently, she shook her head.

"I love you."

She narrowed her eyes. "You lied to me. Do you think you're the first hunter to target my father for a mythical cure? Somehow you made me believe you were my..."

Mate.

She didn't finish the sentence, but she didn't need to.

Without another word, she turned her back on me and stormed from the cell. I hung my head, staring at the dried patches of blood on the dirt as failure after failure stacked upon my shoulders.

I'd failed everyone I'd ever loved.

Layla

Hours later, I stood in front of the entrance to the cell as darkness caved in on me from all sides, seeping into my bones, slowly extinguishing the light.

Wyatt had lied to me. Trey had deceived me.

I'd called my father, told him everything. He'd arrive within the hour. By that time, Wyatt would be gone. Trey had already fled, having bolted during the fight with Baker, and Deakin swore he knew nothing of Trey's plans. It didn't matter. Once word reached the other packs, Trey would have nowhere to run. My father had a lot of allies.

Knots tightened in my stomach. I knew what I needed to do, but part of me struggled to step back inside the cells.

Love someone and set them free. I'd never understood that expression until now. When having your loved one close caused more pain than good, setting them free was the only option.

Love.

Part of me wanted so badly to believe Wyatt. I wanted to trust his words, but doubt was a real killer. It ate away at my logic and fed it to the blackness trickling into my heart.

As teenagers, Trey would joke about us mating in the future. But I'd never felt more than friendship toward him. I'd never felt anything remotely to how I feel for...

My heart squeezed.

Trey had craved the alpha position so desperately that he was willing to kill my father to have it. But he forgot one crucial factor: he needed me, not my father. Trey couldn't lead the pack without me. Even if I took him as a life mate, he'd lead the pack *with* me, not instead of me.

He probably never anticipated me finding my fated mate. Quiet, reserved Layla, the pack's healer, the naïve shifter who craved peace. Trey could never compare to Wyatt. In the short time I'd known Wyatt, he'd been gentle, protective, loving. He'd saved my life and shown me pleasure beyond my wildest dreams.

He'd shown me the stars from the palm of his hand.

Heaviness weighed on my chest.

I loved him. It didn't matter that he was a hunter. It also didn't matter that he'd originally come to Timber Falls hoping for a cure. This war had subjected us both to a world of hatred and bloodshed. For what? Control? Dominance? Supremacy over other species?

No one fought for peace.

No one.

Clarity seeped into my veins as I steadied my breath and stepped into the cave. I rolled the vial in my hand before slipping it into my pocket, descending the steps to Wyatt's cell. Yellowish bruises covered his jawline, most of the visible injuries already healed, including his eye. Whatever Trey had injected him with was wearing off.

I sensed his growing power in my blood, it hummed in my soul like another layer of skin coating mine. When his head lifted and his gaze locked with mine, my breath stalled.

How, in such a short period of time, could this man have changed my life?

I halted a few steps away from him, my wolf purred, curling up in a ball just from being near him. I'd never felt so betrayed by everyone, including my wolf.

"I didn't think you'd come back."

Moving behind him, I unlocked the manacles from his wrist, letting them fall to the floor.

"Thank you." He grunted, rolling his shoulders before standing.

He swayed a bit and I reached for him, only to think better of it and step back.

"Layla, I know my initial intention to use you to get to the pack wasn't...ideal. I can't do anything about that. But I stayed for you. I said that witches don't believe in mates, but I believe in fate. Fate led me to you."

That sharp pain returned to my heart, piercing it with an invisible dagger. I swallowed it all, locking my emotions in a steel cage. "Fate led you to me for a different reason." I dug the vial from my pocket and held it out for him. "This is what you came for, what you wanted. It's my father's blood. I keep a vial in my medical kit for emergencies, when a pack member's wounds are too severe, and my father can't get to them quickly enough. It's been in my cabin the entire time." I pushed it into his hand. "Take it."

He peered at the vial.

"If you believe you can create a cure with my father's blood, then it's yours."

He shook his head. "I don't want it, Layla." He inched closer again, and I didn't have the strength to tell him to stop. "I was wrong, I know that. I want to make this right. I want to be with you. I can control the blood-lust around you."

Tears burned my eyes. "Don't you see? What we have is nothing but lies. All I've ever wanted was peace and I thought with you, we could achieve that. But I was wrong. There'll never be an end to the fighting."

This time when he reached for me, I stepped back.

Tears threatened to fall as I shook my head. "Take it. Leave Timber Falls and never come back."

"I'm not leaving you."

"I'm not asking." A tear slipped free. "For what it's worth, I do believe fate sent you to me. You showed me magic beyond my comprehension. You opened my eyes and filled my heart. I'll always be thankful for that. But this is where it ends."

Before I changed my mind, I turned and walked away, leaving my heart on the cold, bloodied dirt by his feet.

chapter twenty-three

Layla

"Where is it?" I grumbled to the vacant room for the umptieth time.

My butt was numb, my eyes blurry, but my mind was still wide-awake searching for the clue. The evidence I needed. I'd sat on the carpet, surrounded by ancient texts strewn across the floor, for what seemed like days. Daylight had come and gone for the second time, and still I hadn't found it. I'd called Mia a million times, trying to decipher words and spells.

Was I going mad?

As a pup, I used to sneak into this room and read these texts, reciting laws from the ancient packs. Though things had changed over the years, the fundamentals remained. I learned about the hunter curse and the witches who created it from these books, and the stories in here made me first wonder about the possibility of peace.

I was not using this research as a coping mechanism. Not one bit. Nor was I using it to avoid thinking about

Wyatt and how I'd ordered him to leave. I'd given him a vial of my father's blood, knowing it wouldn't cure the curse, and told him to never come back.

I couldn't think of it without the pain inside my chest roaring to life. Even though I'd shifted since he'd left, my wolf still paced inside my mind, clawing, growling as though she'd never forgive me.

Maybe I wouldn't either.

I'd found my mate, sealed our bond, then sent him on his way. No potion or spell could repair the emptiness in my soul.

I hung my head as the pages blurred.

"Sweet pea, why are you still awake?"

I startled, glancing up to find my father standing in the doorway.

"I just need a few more minutes." *Hours. Days.*

He stepped into the room, scanning the mess. "Tell me what you're looking for."

I'd confessed everything to him, including how I harbored a hunter in my cabin and how Wyatt had saved my life when the other hunter attacked. I didn't tell him that he was my mate. Why bother? I suspected he already knew. Shifters could sense a mate bond, alphas even more so.

I thought I'd found love like my parents had. Like my father spoke of. Even though my mother had died while birthing me, which wasn't uncommon amongst shifters, my father had never taken another. He'd told me his heart and soul belonged to my mother and her alone. No one could replace her. I often wondered if that were true, or if the reason he didn't take another was because he refused to diminish her memory for me. But now I knew better. He was right. Nothing could even come close to replicating a mate bond. And now I'd experienced a sliver of that feeling, it created a dull ache that would never disappear.

A tear slipped down my cheek.

"I don't blame you for healing the hunter. I'd think something was wrong if you let the male die knowing you could've helped. Your compassion, your strength of character is what will make you a great alpha."

I couldn't look at him, not yet, not until I had control of my emotions. I peered back at the texts. "I thought there was something in here about...a cure."

He didn't speak for the longest time. "For the hunter curse?"

I nodded.

When he remained silent again, I lifted my gaze. Big mistake. He saw right through me.

"I never told you this." He dragged a chair out from behind the antique mahogany desk and sat. "Your mother craved peace once, almost as much as you do. She and Joan Whitcome used to spend hours scouring grimoires, searching for the tiniest clue that could end the bloodlust."

"What? Why didn't you ever tell me?"

His shoulders drooped. "They never found it. And everything they thought was a lead, turned out to be false. You can't cure him, Layla. I know you want to, but sometimes, a person, whether it be a shifter or a...witch, is beyond healing. You can't save everyone."

"He didn't choose this path." The words stuck in my throat.

"Not many hunters do, but once they cross that line and activate the curse, they can't transform back."

I shook my head. "I saw it. He fought the bloodlust. He'd never hurt me."

I grabbed a text, flipping through the pages, refusing to believe it. Something tickled the back of my memory, clawing at me to remember. I'd read these texts front to back, filling my knowledge with potions and ancient healing methods. Maybe I was wrong, maybe it was a fairytale I created in my head. But until I knew for sure, until I exhausted every avenue, I wouldn't give up.

"Layla, stop." Defeat softened my father's voice. "The only clue your mother found related to direct descendants of the original coven. Not all hunters. Only a select few."

I stared at the text on the floor beside me, open to the page where it listed the ten original families.

Eloise and Wyatt Hale.

Ellie. Wyatt's sister.

Outside the cells, Trey had mentioned how the original families were powerful even as hunters. At the time, it hadn't clicked into place. But now...

Wyatt Hale.

He was a descendent from the original coven of witches.

My heart almost died right there. That explained why he could still access his power even though the curse infected his blood. That explained why his sister was so powerful.

My finger smoothed along the dark script on the faded, yellowing parchment.

"Wyatt Hale."

I looked up at my father, my racing pulse making me nauseous. "Tell me. Tell me what she found."

He crouched on the floor, scanning the texts until he found the right one. He flicked through the pages before holding it open for me. I couldn't decipher the words, but the pictures were enough. They depicted a half man/half wolf, standing on two legs. Time had distorted the drawing, but I could make out a wolf snout and ears, with human-like limbs. A shifter. The other beside it was of a female witch. Surrounding them...stars.

A colorless version of the same stars Wyatt had shown me in the cave.

I didn't get it—

I gasped.

Right there, on the page. Blood dripped from twin puncture marks in the shifter's neck. A matching drop at the corner of the witch's chin.

"Alpha," I murmured.

Wyatt wasn't the first hunter searching for alpha blood to cure the curse, I just thought it wouldn't work.

"Not exactly. Over the centuries, the word was lost in translation. But your mother and Joan believed it meant something like unequaled, primal, powerful. They never thought it meant alpha." My father pointed to the picture of the shifter. "She thought it referred to a fated mate. That drinking blood from a fated mate would cure the curse."

My heart thudded. Could it be?

He straightened. "Layla, I've never heard of it being successful. The bloodlust takes control, and the hunter always ends up killing the shifter."

I thought of Mia and Noah. But no one really knew whether Noah's shifter blood cured the hunter curse in Mia or whether she never turned because they'd already sealed their mate bond.

Wyatt had drunk my blood before we sealed the mate bond. First, he'd taken a small taste when I cut my finger, then he'd bitten my wrist when I'd returned from patrol. Could he control the craving because we were fated mates? Was he already cured?

"He's my...mate."

Silence again.

"I...told him to leave."

I twisted to face my father. He tilted his head, studying me. Sometimes, I wished I knew what he was thinking.

Everything I'd bottled up over the past week bubbled to the surface. "I thought the pack wouldn't accept him, not after the recent attacks. I did what I thought was right. I put the pack first."

He placed a comforting hand on my shoulder. "Is that what you wanted? For him to leave?"

I shook my head. It hurt too much. Why would I ever want this?

"You're so much like your mother."

I scoffed and stood, pacing the room. "Yeah right. She would never heal a hunter, hide it from her family, from her pack, and then let the hunter escape."

A soft smile lightened his expression as though he

knew a secret. "You saved a life, found your mate, and prioritized the safety of your pack. Sounds a lot like your mother to me."

I stopped mid-step.

"The only thing your mother would've done differently is have faith in me, and her pack, to accept her mate."

"He's a hunter."

"He's your mate. Despite what led him to Timber Falls, he protected my daughter and saved her life."

I stared at the man who resembled my father yet spoke words like one of the heroes in the romance books I read. In the short time we'd been together, Wyatt had protected me, he'd saved my life.

"Where is he now?"

"I don't know." I threw my hands in the air. "I was so stupid. I gave him your blood and told him to leave."

My father frowned. "Why would you do that? My blood won't cure him."

I laughed as hysteria set in.

My father stood and wrapped an arm around my shoulder drawing me in. "I can't make any promises, but we can...try. If the cure doesn't work, we'll try something else. Just don't let this consume you."

Before I asked why, something flashed out of the corner of my eye outside the window. Was it Wyatt? Had he come back?

I stepped toward the window and scanned the darkness. Someone was out there, I sensed it.

Just when I thought I'd imagined it, my father growled at the same time the automatic porch light flicked on. My heart thudded for a different reason. Trey stood on the manicured lawn. His deadly glare lifted to the window I looked from, and I quickly ducked out of sight.

My father moved closer, waves of alpha power rolling off his shoulders.

"Rhett St. Claire," Trey bellowed. "I challenge you for territory."

chapter twenty-four

Wyatt

I paced back and forth in the cave, wearing a track in the dirt just as I had for the last two days. The vial of alpha blood tormented me, burning a hole in my hand. *Use it. Don't use it.* What the hell did I do?

If I used the blood, it might cure the bloodlust, but it meant I was no better than all other hunters who'd attacked innocent shifter packs searching for a cure. Well, that wasn't true. Most hunters couldn't give two shits about a cure, the bloodlust had already overtaken to the point of no return. All they craved was shifter blood to feed the gnawing hunger in their guts.

If I didn't take it, I risked becoming one of them permanently.

I'd balanced on the edge for so many days, it wouldn't take much longer for the bloodlust to control my every thought. Then, I'd lose those last threads of my humanity. Did I still have them?

I'd killed for blood. I'd killed to avenge Ellie.

I'd killed for the cure.

How much longer until I killed for the thrill?

I rolled the vial in my hand, staring at the dark crimson liquid sloshing in the glass.

Take it. Don't take it.

I'd come to Timber Falls searching for a cure. To prevent others from turning into the monster Ellie had. To finish this, so her death wasn't for nothing.

But when I'd stumbled on the small town, I'd found something much more enticing. Someone who filled the void in my soul that I hadn't realized was there. Layla had said I helped her see the universe through fresh eyes, yet she'd done the same for me.

Not all shifters were monsters. Not all of them killed hunters for sport.

Her dreams of peace had planted a seed of hope inside me. Could we coexist?

Could she...love a monster?

Could we have a future?

I peered at the jagged rock above my head remembering our night here. I possessed all the magic in the world, more power than I ever needed, and still, I didn't have the answers.

The sound of a pebble skipping off the rockface echoed in the tunnels outside the cave. I switched off the lantern and stashed the vial in my pocket. Darkness filled the cavern, and I blinked until my eyes adjusted. With my back flush against the wall, I inched closer to the cave's entrance. No one knew I was here. When Layla told me to leave Timber Falls, this was the first place I thought of going. A place to hide while I figured out what to do.

Besides, until recently, I'd never allowed myself to stop moving.

When I'd left here last time, I intended to hunt down the traitor and end his ass, only he'd blind-sided me first. I wouldn't make that mistake again. I planned to take that asshole's soul to hell along with me.

Heavy footsteps pounded closer, so damn loud the culprit clearly had no idea someone else was inside the caves or they didn't care. Either way, I held deadly still and...waited.

Layla had said only Baker and her knew about this cave. That didn't mean someone else hadn't discovered it over the years.

Layla.

Did she come here seeking solace in the caves, like me? Seeking a space that reminded her of a snippet in time where we were only Layla and Wyatt, not enemies, not standing on different sides of a war. Did she want to remember the moment where our lives collided?

The moment she gave herself to me and I to her.

The hollowness in my chest reared its ugly head again, but I buried it.

I inhaled, sifting through the scents as the footsteps drew nearer. Dirt, moss, leather, and cheap cologne. Male. Probably a shifter, given the cocky stride, but I couldn't tell, especially if they took the same concoction Layla did to mask her scent.

The footsteps curved around the entrance of the cave. I braced myself for a fight wishing like hell I had a weapon. Anything would do. Instead, I'd make do with the element of surprise and sheer strength.

The shadowy figure slowed their steps as they entered the cave, with their back to me. I couldn't identify them in the darkness. I had less than a second and didn't waste it. I shot forward, snagging the intruder around the neck in a headlock. The guy elbowed my ribs with one arm and clawed at my forearm with his other hand. I tightened my hold, sweeping my leg to knock him off balance. It didn't work. He kicked my knee sending wicked pain up my leg. My vision sharpened, and I braced for the hunter side of me to rise.

No, not now.

A low growl built in the guy's chest. "Wyatt..."

Clarity seeped into my brain.

Baker.

I loosened my hold, and Baker shoved off me, spinning to face me. "You're fucking lucky I don't kick your ass for that."

"Like you could." I sneered at him. "Next time, don't surprise a hunter."

Dumbass.

Thinking of Layla insinuating it, brought a smile to my face. I switched the lantern back on, flooding the cave with light.

Baker eyed the sleeping bag and backpack beside the lantern. "I wondered who stole my gear."

I shrugged, making no apology for swiping the supplies from the back of his truck. I'd made do over the years bouncing from place to place but sleeping on the dirt in a damp cave was a whole new level of low for me.

"Why are you here?" I asked, crossing my arms.

Baker shot me a hard stare. "I could ask you the same thing."

We stood there glaring at each other like an old-school cowboy standoff minus the weapons. And cowboy hats.

Eventually, I broke the awkwardness. "Layla told me to leave, and I told her I wouldn't."

His gaze dipped to the ground before lifting again.

I stepped forward. "Wait. Is she all right? Did something happen? Has someone killed the fucking traitor yet?"

His mouth lifted in the corner with a faint smile as he shoved his hands in his jean pockets. "For a hunter, you're all right."

I almost said the same about him but held back. Feeding egos wasn't my thing.

"Listen, I'm Layla's biggest fan, I've protected her my entire—"

A quiver rippled through my blood, followed by a heavy sense of dread. I rubbed my sternum.

Baker frowned. "What's wrong?"

"It's like..." The feeling of dread sank lower in my gut, swirling around until it curled into a wild mess. My heartrate kicked up, not enough to alert of danger or prepare to fight, just the slightest notch to suggest something was wrong. As though something set my hunter side on red alert.

I cocked my ear toward the entrance to the cave, lowering my voice. "Anyone follow you?"

Baker stiffened, inching ever so quietly to the

entrance. He waited several heartbeats before shaking his head.

If no one else was in the cave, why did my body want to flee?

I closed my eyes, concentrating on the sensations. They fired around inside me, but not stemming from one point as though they weren't entirely mine...Layla.

I must've said it aloud because Baker spun. "Can you sense her?"

Her blood.

Her blood ran through my veins, I'd used it to track her to the bookshop. Only now, fear laced the connection.

"She's in trouble."

Baker caught on quick. "She's at her father's."

Without waiting, I darted down the tunnels following our connection, hoping I found her in time.

chapter twenty-five

Layla

Trey.

Just thinking his name made me want to vomit. The traitor who planned to kill my father and somehow convince me to mate with him so he could lead the Timber Falls pack. That same fiery rage as before bubbled inside my blood. He'd kidnapped my mate and threatened his life. He'd blackmailed me. He'd used me to further his own agenda.

And now he stood on my parents' lawn, challenging my father for territory.

My father clutched my shoulders, turning me to face him. "Control the shift, Layla. Remain in human form and stay inside the house."

"He can't challenge you for Timber Falls, he's not even an alpha."

His steady hand squeezed my shoulder. "Regardless, I won't stand down from a challenge. Not from Trey or any other shifter who seeks to take over this pack. This is our pack. Our family. And we protect what's ours."

My heart sliced into pieces. *We protect what's ours.*

Wyatt.

I hadn't protected him, I'd sent him away.

I forced the thought aside. I couldn't think about that right now, not when I needed to focus. Trey had challenged my father. The surviving wolf would control Timber Falls. This was the one pack law I wished someone had abolished.

When I nodded, my father silently exited the room.

I inhaled a deep breath, sending a promise to my wolf that she'd have her opportunity soon.

I backed toward the door.

I couldn't let Trey do this. He wanted Timber Falls so badly that when his plan to mate with me failed, he resorted to challenging my father. Out of pride? Or stupidity? Was power and control worth dying for?

To Trey, maybe.

And I had a feeling he wouldn't challenge my father without a few tricks up his sleeve. He'd worked with hunters.

Mind made up, I raced out of the room, down the hall, taking the stairs two at a time, exiting through the back door. The cool night air awakened my senses. Awareness buzzed inside me, my wolf fighting the shift, caught in that strange place where I was half wolf, half human. With heightened hearing, I tracked every creak in the floorboards on the porch while sifting through the air, identifying nearby wolves.

Trey, my father, and two other pack members.

Three potential enemies. So far.

Something raw and wild swelled in my blood as I

slipped around the corner of the house, crouching behind the porch railing. Through the slates, I had a perfect view of Trey, and I was close enough that my wolf could attack in an instant.

Trey stood in only a pair of jeans, feet shoulder-width apart, his fists clenching and unclenching. The bruises from where he'd fought Baker still visible over his bare chest and face. For a hot second, I felt sad for him. What had happened for him to resort to challenging my father? If he'd fled, like Baker and I thought he had, he might've lived.

A life on the run wasn't ideal, but at least he'd live.

Now, there was no guarantee he'd even have that.

My father descended the porch steps, halting on the lawn a few paces from Trey. Even from where I crouched, I sensed the alpha energy rolling off him in waves.

"Leave Timber Falls, Trey. Leave now and I'll forget you challenged me for a position that isn't yours to take."

Trey held his ground. "Your time is up, old man."

My wolf fought harder, desperate to protect her alpha, to protect my father.

"What do you hope to achieve? You think my daughter will stomach the sight of you after you kill her father?"

Trey was delusional. I could never love him, not even with the years between us. My heart had never considered him more than a friend and now I knew why. It had been waiting for Wyatt.

My mate.

I wouldn't let Trey do this.

I stood, moving out from behind the porch. My pulse quickened as I stepped into the porch light flooding the grass.

Trey's gaze darted to mine.

A sickening smile curled on his lips. "Last chance, Layla. Become my life mate and your father lives."

I shook my head. What a joke. Even if I agreed, Trey wouldn't let my father survive. I had to trust my father would win, that he'd defeat Trey. I wanted to look at him, but if I did, I knew his dark gaze would flick to me and Trey would take advantage of his distraction.

All I'd ever wanted was peace, and Trey had destroyed that by bringing war to our doorstep. Those hunters had killed our pack members. And now, he challenged my father and sought to destroy my family.

Enough.

My feet gravitated closer. Heat flashed through my blood, singing with power.

Tonight, I wouldn't sit on the sidelines any longer. I'd take a stand, not only for this town, but for all shifters. For peace.

Wyatt

Closing my eyes, I focused on the blood connection to Layla and directed Baker as he drove the truck like a mad man. I wiped my sweaty palms on my jeans. I never should've left. I should've fought harder for her. I should've stayed to protect her, even from the shadows.

Worry and unease collided in my gut. Bile rose in my throat.

If someone hurts her...

Baker swore and I opened my eyes.

"She's still at her father's house."

The truck skidded to a halt somewhere in the forest. I didn't bother to find out where, Layla was here, close. I threw open the passenger door.

Baker rounded the hood. "Layla's here, and Rhett. So is fucking Trey." He lifted his nose in the air. "There are at least two other shifters, but I have no way of knowing if they're siding with Trey or Rhett."

I couldn't smell the shifters, no doubt because they took the same concoction masking their scent.

"Give me the layout of the estate."

Baker pointed ahead. "House is through there. Two levels, three entrances. One from the front and two from the rear."

I nodded.

Baker narrowed his eyes. "Trey's the enemy here, not anyone else until we confirm it."

He didn't trust me. I didn't blame him, nor did I care. Instead, I leveled him with a harsh glare. "If someone hurts Layla, I make no apology for ripping them to shreds. Enemy or not."

Without waiting, I bolted toward the house hoping that once the bloodlust consumed me, I could distinguish between enemies and allies.

Racing through the woods, I welcomed the flood of fire through my blood, the rush of it, the heightened senses. How my vision sharpened, yet it didn't narrow nor tint with amber. But I didn't question the change.

A wolf came out of nowhere, launching at me from the side.

I spun just in time, the wolf's jaws narrowly missing me. Another wolf, white as snow, attacked the first. They rolled and tumbled, jaws snapping at each other. Assuming the white wolf was Baker, I left to find Layla.

Breaching the tree line, I skidded to a halt.

On the lawn in front of Layla's family home, two wolves snarled, teeth bared as they circled each other. A large gray wolf and a smaller, no less vicious, black one. Slightly back, a reddish-grey wolf growled, crouched low, searching for an opening.

Layla.

I'd never seen her wolf, but I felt the connection.

A vision slammed my mind so hard and fast, my knees buckled. Wolves. Blood. Snarling and the sickening sounds of tearing flesh. Ellie's screams.

I gagged. Fever swept through me.

Not again.

I couldn't let another person I loved die. I had to stop Layla, to do something. Straightening, I focused on the two wolves, but I couldn't fucking tell who they were. Friend or foe? Ally or enemy?

I inched closer, scanning for an opening or a weapon.

A dagger lay by a pile of shredded clothes, and I almost laughed. I darted toward it, but Layla intercepted. She snapped at my heels, forcing me back.

"I'm here to help."

Her wolf didn't like that response. She growled louder, all defiant, snapping at my shins. Little did she know, she'd met her match in me. I'd spent the last few decades hunting for a cure, taking on shifters far more vicious than her.

Bold was my middle name. Or dumbass, we'd know for sure shortly.

Another wolf yelped, and Layla spun.

The black one had his jaws clenched around the gray one's throat, thrashing its head back and forth. Before I could stop her, Layla launched at the black wolf, latching onto his hind leg.

Now, I knew which one was Traitor Trey.

Bracing my feet on the earth, I held out my hands, summoning the ancient power vibrating beneath my skin. It roared to life. Gusts of wind swept across the space, whirling around the fight, lifting dried leaves and small twigs into the air. Narrowing my focus, I twisted the whirlwind into shadowy ropes, coiling them around the traitorous wolf.

Magic came easier, fiercer than ever before.

Layla thrashed at the wolf's leg, but the asshole didn't stop. He tore at the other wolf's throat. I yanked the ropes tighter, constricting Turd's midsection, crunching ribs.

Douchebag released his jaws with a yelp but spun to bite Layla.

It felt as though time slowed. The injured gray wolf lunged. At the same time, dickwad shifted into human form and swiped the blade off the grass. Layla, oblivious to the knife, attacked from behind. Trey spun, ready to strike.

The need to protect her amplified a surge of power.

I'd intended to kill him when I left Layla, but he'd gotten to me first. That wouldn't happen again.

My lips curled back, baring my fangs. In one swift move, I released the ropes and launched at Trey, slamming my fangs into his neck. I vaguely registered a howl, followed by a shout. I didn't care.

Shifter blood filled my mouth as I tore a giant hole in his flesh—

Bad. The blood tasted off.

I gagged, shoving the asshole away. Trey's lifeless body toppled to the ground by my feet. I spat the blood on the dirt, coughing and retching, trying to expel it from my mouth. Something was wrong.

Layla cried out. I wiped my mouth, staggering to where she crouched on the ground.

Blood smeared her face and naked flesh.

I lowered beside her. "Where are you hurt?"

"Not me."

As though my brain could only cope with one scene at a time, my gaze landed on the motionless wolf beneath her hands. A knife protruded from the wolf's throat.

Before I could stop her, Layla yanked out the dagger. Blood gushed from the wound, a steady flow onto the grass.

"Shift," she cried out. "Shift, Father. Shift."

In a blur of motion, the wolf shifted into human form, but it didn't stop the bleeding. It made it worse. Layla pressed her hands over the wound, but blood seeped around them.

My heart sank. This was Layla's father. The alpha I'd hunted.

The blood seeping into the earth by my knees would cure my curse.

By the tree line, I sensed a hunter bolt toward us, no doubt drawn by the blood. I flicked my hand toward it, curling ropes of wind around the hunter's legs. A second later, Baker's wolf launched from behind, tearing at the hunter's neck. This much blood would attract more hunters loitering in the area.

Layla shoved her wrist in front of me. "Use the knife to open my vein. He can't heal on his own. He'll die before I get to a medic kit."

When I swiped the dagger from the ground, tiny pulses of sickening power jittered through my fingers. I flung it behind me.

"Don't touch the knife."

She shoved me aside to reach for it, but I snagged her wrist. "Layla, it's spelled with dark magic. I can feel it pulsing in my hand."

Tears streamed down her face. "He planned this. Trey planned to kill him all along. My father needs blood."

I understood more than she realized. If she didn't heal her father soon, my hunter side would take over and I'd kill him instead.

"Wyatt. Now." She held out her wrist again. "Use your fangs. My blood is the closest to alpha blood. Hurry."

I stared at her wrist, then back at her father lying in a pool of his own blood. His features were paler, his chest convulsing. He didn't have long.

This moment felt like a turning point in my destiny.

Saving this wolf, her father, wouldn't atone for all the lives I'd taken. It also wouldn't magically change how Layla and I descended from two different worlds. But... maybe it was a step in the right direction. A step toward cleansing my soul.

I wanted to try harder to control the bloodlust. I'd learn to identify the signs earlier and perhaps develop an immunity to it. For her, I'd try anything. She made me want to step out of the shadows and live again.

I wanted to be a worthy mate. I wanted her heart and her soul for the rest of our lives.

Before I knew what I'd done, I removed the vial from inside my pocket. My hand tightened around it.

This was Layla's father.

I popped the lid.

On the other side of the lawn, the white wolf shimmered and shifted back into human form. Baker, covered in gashes and puncture wounds. A dead hunter lay at his feet. The guy resembled me a week ago, having fought these same shifters. The only difference was Layla had saved me. If she hadn't, I wouldn't be here now, crouching before a shifter, fighting my hunter instincts to save him.

I could never repay her for healing me, but this was a damn good start.

I wouldn't let her suffer as I had when I lost Ellie.

Without another thought, I whirled the air around the wound, holding the skin together to pause the bleeding. Leaning over her father, I poured the alpha blood inside his mouth.

Layla cried out, her voice raspy, full of pain, and all I

wanted to do was wrap her in my arms and shield her from this forever. Baker bolted to us, falling to his knees on the other side of her dad.

"I'll fucking kill Trey all over again for this," he growled.

I had the urge to say I'd beat him to it, but now didn't feel like the right time to joke.

Instead, I stared at the ugly tear in her father's neck. I couldn't heal it properly without herbs.

For the past few decades, hell, a few days ago, I'd only craved shifter blood. Yet now, I felt nothing but numbness.

Shivers racked my body. I recalled my power and backed away as the blood flow eased to a trickle. I couldn't help any longer. All I could do was hope to the stars the blood worked its magic. Hope. An emotion so foreign I didn't even know what it felt like anymore.

chapter twenty-six

Layla

The bed dipped as I sat down on the side, taking my father's hand in mine. After the wound in his neck began to heal, Baker carried him upstairs to his room, and he'd slept ever since.

I hadn't spoken to Wyatt. Not about his return, him killing Trey, or about how he used his magic and the vial of alpha blood to save my father. I wasn't sure where I'd even start.

Dark stains seeped through the gauze around my father's neck, but his pulse was steady. He'd live.

Wyatt had saved him.

In hindsight, perhaps saving my father was his way of repaying me for saving him. All we'd done over the past week was save each other. I'd been wrong earlier when I said our bond was based on lies. It was based on trust. And devotion.

I sensed Baker appear in the doorway, taking in the room for a few seconds before moving to the other side of the bed.

"How's he doing?"

"Good." My throat was all scratchy. I wanted to cry, but the tears wouldn't fall. "Wyatt saved him. If he hadn't..."

After a quiet moment, Baker spoke. "He sensed something was wrong. As though he felt the mate connection and knew you were in danger. I don't know how it's possible for him to feel it, but I swear he did."

Maybe that same connection was what drew him to my porch in the beginning. I was so stupid to believe a word of what Trey had said. Baker was right, no one could fake a mate bond. Not the connection nor the feelings. Even if Wyatt had come to Timber Falls with the intention to take alpha blood, I suspect finding each other had skewed his objectives.

I stayed for you.

"Did he...leave?"

Baker shook his head. "He's outside on the porch. I think the rest of the pack doesn't quite know what the hell to do with him."

I'd alerted the entire pack once Baker and I had stabilized my father. They needed to know what had happened. Deakin plus another had sided with Trey last night, and Baker had killed them.

Three more dead pack members.

My father's eyes fluttered behind his closed lids, and I gave his hand a gentle squeeze.

Wyatt had saved him. And he was outside right now, waiting for me.

I stayed for you.

My gaze found Baker's from across the bed. "I need to..."

He nodded. "Go. I'll stay with your father."

Swallowing the lump in my throat, I kissed my father's hand before laying it by his side.

On my way, I swung past the study to collect the grimoire before taking the back stairs to avoid questions from the pack. I'd update them after I'd spoken with Wyatt. Outside, I found him with his forearms braced on the banister, peering out toward the forest. Someone had given him new clothes, and the look sent my heart racing. Dark jeans, form-fitting back T-shirt. His jet-black hair was a complete mess, thick strands going in all different directions. I wanted so badly to run my fingers through it while he kissed me.

As I opened the screen door, he straightened and turned my way. Our gazes locked, and I felt as though the ground shifted beneath my feet.

"Hey." I sank down on the porch swing and patted the space beside me.

He shoved his hands in his pockets. "Is your father...alive?"

"Yes. Thanks to you."

He gravitated closer. My heart bounced around behind my ribs. "If you hadn't used your magic or given him the blood when you did..." My throat tightened again, cutting off the words.

He crouched between my legs, taking my hands in his.

"I gave that blood to you. Why did you use it to heal my father?"

Logic told me the answer, but I needed to hear him say it. I needed to know where we stood.

"It wasn't even a choice, Layla." His thumb drew tiny circles on the back of my hands. "I've never taken the easy road in life. I'll beat the bloodlust. I want to beat it, for you."

A lump expanded in the back of my throat.

Wyatt's gaze dipped to the grimoire on the cushion beside me. He stood. "Why do you have my family's grimoire?"

My eyes widened. "What did you say?"

"That crest. It's my family's."

I brushed my fingers over the tarnished bronze twisted vines encircling what looked like a raven. "A witch, Joan Whitcome from Woodland Falls, gave this to my mother decades ago, before I was even born."

"Joan Whitcome." He said the name with a hint of familiarity.

"Did you know her?"

He sank onto the porch swing beside me, his long legs kicking us off on a gentle rock. I easily slipped into imagining our future, of us sitting on this porch for years to come, curled up in each other's arms.

He held out his hand, and I passed him the grimoire, watching as he flipped through the pages until he found the one he wanted. He lifted it slightly, showing me. On the faded parchment was the same list of names I'd read hundreds of times.

"The Whitcomes are one of the original families. Part of the original coven." His finger moved two names over. "So are the Hales. My family. This book went missing decades ago after my parents hid it from Ellie." His gaze lifted to me. "You've had it this entire time."

Maybe fate had sent him to me after all.

Hang on. Decades? I knew hunters, just like shifters, aged at a much slower rate than humans, but exactly how old was Wyatt? Not that it mattered. Age was just a number in our world.

I scooted closer, leaning over to turn the pages. "Here, on this page, it refers to the hunter curse, the bloodlust and..." I looked at him as my stomach fluttered. "The cure."

"Taking blood from an alpha. I already knew that."

"No." I swallowed as my breath bottled in my chest. "My mother and Joan spent years deciphering the spell. They didn't think it was alpha blood. They think the cure is blood from a fated mate."

He frowned, reading the page, flipping back and forth as though double-checking the text. "But..." He stared at the page, then back at me. "I don't understand. Witches don't believe in fated mates. How could the cure rely on them finding one?"

"The original curse was because witches wanted to defeat shifters, but instead, they unintentionally created hunters. A curse that's plagued witches ever since, from all over the globe." I entwined my fingers with his. "Everything you said about balance makes sense. Of course, the cure would involve a shifter and a witch because the curse did. But not an alpha. The cure depends on a pairing that joins the two worlds together in peace."

He leaned back, searching my eyes. "Your blood.

That's why when I...incapacitated Douchebag, his blood tasted off. As though I couldn't stomach it. That's why my vision didn't change." He glanced back at the text, trailing his finger down the lines, and flipped over the page. "The cure doesn't take away the hunter aspects it... cures the bloodlust. That's why I still have fangs."

Heat rippled through my middle as he ran his tongue over one. "I'm, um, okay if you keep them. I kind of like your fangs."

His finger stilled as he side-eyed me. "Do you now?" His voice was deep and smoky, sending a thrill right between my legs.

I nodded. Best not to speak in case I squeaked.

"That's fortunate because to maintain my awesome powers and heightened senses, I should probably take a little blood from my mate each day."

I cleared my throat. "Absolutely, that sounds like a sensible idea."

His damn dimples chose that moment to make a full appearance, and if I weren't sitting down, my legs would've buckled.

Placing the grimoire beside him, Wyatt leaned in to hover his mouth at my ear. "I can think of a number of veins I haven't tasted you from yet." His wicked tongue licked my neck and I all but combusted. "Maybe we'll try one here." His hand slipped between my legs, trailing up my inside thigh. "Then another one here."

I moaned, sinking farther into the swing, and Wyatt captured my mouth with his. The kiss conveyed everything I hoped for our future, for the cure, for peace. Mainly, I kissed him with all my hope for us.

Before I slid off the swing in a puddle of swoon, Wyatt drew back and lifted my hand between us. His dark hazel gaze found mine. "In all seriousness, what now? What happens with us? I want to be with you, Layla. Whatever it takes." He lifted my hand to his lips, placing a gentle kiss. "I've wandered this world for so long, unknowingly searching for you. I'm not about to walk away."

I cupped his stubbly jaw in my hand. "For so long, all I've wanted was peace. Peace among our kind, between witches and shifters. Together, we can achieve that. Sure, there'll still be danger, not all hunters come from original covens, not all can cure the bloodlust, but together we can usher in a new world."

"What about your pack? Your father?"

The screen door opened, and my father chose that moment to trudge onto the porch.

"Father."

Wyatt stood at the same time I leaped off the porch swing and darted to my father. "Should you be out of bed?"

He dismissed my concern with the wave of his hand. "I wanted to make sure the man who saved my life hadn't left again."

Man, not hunter.

Wyatt stepped forward, placing his hand on the small of my back. "No, sir. With your blessing, I'd like to stick around." He peered down at me, his golden eyes darkening around the rim. "I love you, Layla. I want to stay here and build a life with you, whatever that looks like."

My heart swelled.

Love.

I raised on my toes, cradling his face in my palms. "I love you."

He met me halfway, kissing me with so much love and passion my heart felt ready to burst. Two enemies, fighting on either side of the war between hunters and shifters, had found each other.

My father cleared his throat.

When Wyatt drew back, I lowered my hands, wrapping my arms around him so he couldn't leave even if he wanted.

"In this pack, we honor fated mates, regardless of who or what that resembles." My father nodded. "You'll make a fine mate to stand beside my daughter. And I have faith you'll both lead this pack into a peaceful future." He held out his hand, and Wyatt shook it. "Welcome to Timber Falls. Welcome to my family."

As my father shook hands with Wyatt, I took a second to capture the moment. The moment the alpha of Timber Falls welcomed a hunter into his wolf pack. The moment he accepted my mate.

The beginning of the rest of my life.

Baker stepped onto the porch, halting behind my father. Movement out of the corner of my eye made me turn toward the backyard. My breath caught. The entire pack congregated on the lawn. Adult shifters, their mates, pups.

My family.

"That's for you, my daughter. The pack is honoring your mate bond."

Hand in hand, Wyatt and I stood on the top step,

peering at all the familiar faces. My aunt and uncle, and Baker's brothers stood in front. I wished my mother could've seen this, I wished she knew how much her research made a difference. I wished she was here to share this moment with my father.

As Wyatt and I descended the steps to the gravel pathway, each pack member lowered to one knee, bowing their heads in a gesture that stole my breath.

Acceptance.

The pack, *my* pack, accepted Wyatt as easily as my father.

We'd usher in a new wave of change. We could spread the word, find descendants of the original witches, and cure the bloodlust. End this war.

Then, one day, we'd live in peace.

Together.

epilogue

Layla - one week later

"Why am I so nervous?" I whispered to myself as I stared into the mirror.

Today, Wyatt and I would officially become mates. Well, technically that happened in the cave almost two weeks ago but mentioning that to my father was slightly awkward, so we'd pretend today was the day.

In seven short days, the entire pack had banded together to organize a mating ceremony. God, we needed it. It had been so long since there was something happy, something to bring the packs together. Something worth celebrating.

With so much blood and death, sometimes I found it hard to see through the devastation. To find the light.

Wyatt.

He was my light.

Baker's mother had done a wonderful job with my hair, braiding deep yellow ribbon through it, adding tiny daisies here and there. It matched the knee-length sundress I wore. I felt beautiful. My heart ached for my mother though. Even though I'd never met her, I'd always felt her near, wanted to confide in her or to have her hold me in her arms, but today, I yearned for it. I wanted her to see the woman I'd become. I wanted her to be proud.

I waved my hand under my eyes as though that would rid the tears threatening to build.

The bedroom door opened, startling me.

I spun as Wyatt slipped inside, softly latching it behind him.

"What are you doing?" I gaped at him. "You're supposed to wait outside."

His sinful grin made my heart flutter. "I thought I'd sneak a quick rendezvous with my sexy mate before I have to share you with all those shifters." He grimaced. "Your pack is rather large. That many shifters in one place kinda makes me nervous. There's only one other witch out there."

We'd invited Mia from Woodland Falls, a descendent of the Whitcome coven, to represent the witches so we could honor his heritage. She'd also agreed to help us locate descendants from the original families so we could help them cure the bloodlust.

I laughed. "My father invited neighboring packs. So, you aren't, um, having any cravings for shifter blood?"

He prowled forward until only a breath of air separated us. I lifted my chin to maintain eye contact.

"I only have cravings for you." His voice dripped seduction and wicked things.

"Really? What sort of cravings?"

Those dimples appeared again, and I stifled a moan.

"The kind that are inappropriate to perform in front of others." He swept the back of his knuckles along my jaw. "You're so beautiful."

Stepping back slightly, he lifted my hand between us and opened my palm to place a delicate necklace inside it.

"It was my sister's. And my mother's before that. It's been in my family for a really long time."

I trailed my finger along the oval pendant and its exquisite detail. Thin vines woven together in an intricate design with a grayish stone in the center. It reminded me of a more delicate version of the crest on his family's grimoire.

"It's moonstone. It represents happiness, love, new beginnings."

The back of my throat burned with so much emotion.

"My mother would've wanted you to have it."

Wyatt lifted the necklace and moved behind me to secure it around my neck. The instant the pendant touched my skin, a slight tingle warmed the spot.

He returned to stand before me. "I placed a protection spell on it. I know your wolf is a badass, but this will..."

He didn't need to finish the sentence. I knew he wanted to protect me because he'd felt responsible for what had happened to his sister.

I brushed my fingers over the pendant. "I love it."

His head bowed slightly, relief washing over his features. "Good. Now, let's do this so we can get to the next part."

"What exactly does the next part entail?"

He leaned in, snagging my earlobe between his teeth. "Let's just say it requires very little clothing."

Before I could respond, he stepped back and offered the crook of his arm. Without hesitation, I slipped my arm in his and he led me downstairs.

On the porch, at the top of the steps, we paused, and I swept my gaze over the pack members who'd gathered for the ceremony. The Archer pack from Cedar Valley was there, Brax with his arm around Kali, while his brothers chatted away beside them. The Cole pack, Noah standing behind Mia with his arms around her. Liam to the right, with his newborn pup cradled in his arms. Baker surrounded by his family. The emotion running through me at that moment threatened to short-circuit my brain.

My father stepped forward, separating himself from the crowd as we descended the steps and followed the path along the lawn.

Everyone who'd ever mattered to me was here to witness our mating ceremony as the joining of not just two souls, two mates, but two worlds.

Wyatt led us to the long rectangular burgundy rug, spread on the ground beneath a weeping willow, its branches fanning over the guests as though we existed in a cocoon of peace and love.

The shifter who conducted mating ceremonies in the surrounding region, waited patiently with his hands clasped in front of him. Silence fell over the space as Wyatt and I stepped onto the rug.

He took my hands in his, and the world around us faded away. I lost myself in his golden eyes while the warmth streaming through our bond filled my heart until it felt ready to burst. The shifter conducted the ceremony, and I spoke at all the appropriate moments, but all I wanted to do was kiss Wyatt. His gaze never wavered from me, sharing all the unspoken words I sensed through our bond.

Happiness. Devotion. Love.

When the crowd cheered, Wyatt closed the distance between us, cupped my face in his hands and kissed me as though we were the only two people in this world.

———

At some point during the night, someone lit a bonfire and the crowd surrounded it, dancing, drinking, laughing. Mating ceremonies often lasted days. I loved that aspect of it, how shifters would come together to celebrate the joining of two souls, but what I craved tonight wasn't family or reminiscing, I ached for alone time with Wyatt.

Since we'd met, I felt as though we'd done nothing but dodge one danger after the other. I yearned for a night where we could be us, without the fear of the pack rejecting Wyatt, worrying about how my family would react, or if more hunters attacked. Tonight, we'd be a normal mated couple. Wyatt and Layla.

As though he read my mind, Wyatt's arms snaked around my middle, pulling me against him. "Want to get out of here?"

He brushed light kisses over my neck.

"I thought you'd never ask."

After saying our goodbyes, Wyatt took my hand and

led me through the forest back to my cabin. His family's necklace warmed against my chest, almost as though each matriarch were here with us, giving their blessing. I wished I'd known his family. Having grown up in a pack, surrounded by people who cared for me, I would've loved for us to welcome his family into mine. But I guess, in a way, we did anyway. The mating ceremony combined our two worlds and welcomed the Hale family into the Timber Falls pack.

Just as the Cole pack in Woodland Falls welcomed the Whitcome family into theirs.

Peace. We were one step closer to living in a world surrounded by peace rather than bloodshed.

Wyatt squeezed my hand but remained silent as we strolled through the forest as though he too was lost in thought.

Exiting the tree line, my step faulted.

Someone had strung fairy lights along the porch, and a path of lanterns leading to the steps.

I grinned up at Wyatt. "Did you do this?"

One side of his mouth kicked up, and those damn dimples made my knees weak. "With a little help from Baker. That guy's a sappy romantic."

I giggled as he scooped me up and carried me up the stairs to the front door, unlocking the door while he balanced me in his arms.

Inside, he kicked it closed with his boot and lowered my feet to the floor.

He cradled my face in his hands, searching my eyes. "For so long, I was lost. Driven by revenge, searching for a cure. I...I think I used it as an excuse to kill. To rage. To destroy others as they'd destroyed me. Because of that, I lost everything. My family, my home, my life."

My heart ached for him.

"Until you." His thumbs gently stroked my cheeks. "Until I found you."

I leaned into his touch.

"You're my calm, Layla. You're my family. My everything."

I raised on my toes and brushed his lips with mine. "I love you."

Before I drew back, he captured my mouth, kissing me with every emotion he had. I felt it all through our bond. What he said was true. I felt the warmth flooding my chest, how my heart reached for his, how an invisible thread streamed from his soul to mine.

No matter the obstacles we'd face, this kiss promised we'd face them together.

Easing back, Wyatt curled his fingers in mine and led me up the staircase to the loft. Something wrapped in black cloth sat on the corner of the bed. He let go of my hand to unwrap it, revealing an antique dagger.

"This is a ceremonial dagger, one used to fuse a binding spell. Mia found it in her grandmother's belongings."

I couldn't slow my heart, it thudded inside my chest as though trying to break free.

"Before you, I existed in a dark cloud of hate. You woke me from that destruction. You gave me life again." He lifted the dagger between us, balancing it on his open palm. "Witches believe the exchange of blood using this dagger seals the bond, melding two souls to one. In the cave, you gave me all of you, and now I want to do the same. I want to honor the old ways and bind myself to you." He dipped his head so we were eye level. "Will you accept my bond?"

My heart had never felt so complete.

I nodded before my brain even registered. Touching the side of his face, I smiled up at him. "Yes. A million times yes."

Holding my hand, Wyatt sat on the edge of the bed and guided me between his legs. He placed the dagger aside and removed his shirt. I tried not to let all that perfectly crafted goodness distract me. His fingers lifted the hem of my dress, pausing at the tops of my thighs, a silent question in his eyes. When I nodded, he lifted it the rest of the way, letting it flutter to the floor by my feet.

I'd never drunk blood before. Well, that wasn't true. My father had given me his blood once when I fell from a tree as a pup and broke two ribs, puncturing my lung. He'd sped up the healing, but I didn't remember it. I only remember that he'd been there. That was also the moment I realized I wanted to heal shifters.

But this felt different. I sensed taking Wyatt's blood would forever change me. Which was true. According to his beliefs, it'd seal our bond. I wanted this. I wanted to accept all of him.

Wyatt lifted the dagger and sliced a small cut over his heart. A droplet of deep crimson pooled at the surface.

"I'll love you until the end of my days. And then, I'll love you into the next life and the one after that," he whispered, reaching up to brush my cheek. "Take from me, Layla."

His hands locked onto my hips, letting me set my own pace while at the same time, holding me tight. His thumbs pushed into my sides shooting wicked bolts of heat between my legs. Inhaling a shaky breath, I leaned forward and trailed my tongue over the cut, drawing a low, almost feral rumble from Wyatt.

Dark, rich blood exploded on my tongue, like a full-bodied wine that had aged in a hidden cave for centuries. I wanted to bottle it. To taste it every day for the rest of my life. Heated shivers danced up and down my spine. Starting at the back of my neck, a magical tingle spread through my veins and across my flesh as his blood fused with mine, consuming every part of me.

Including the heat pooling between my legs.

I drew back, more than a little breathless as the cut healed.

Wyatt lifted the dagger, pausing with the tip just above my breast in the same spot he'd cut himself. "Forever."

Countless gold flecks reflected in his eyes, sparkling back at me like glass caught in the sunlight. I'd never been so sure of something. Never wanted something more than this. "Forever."

I shuddered as the dagger nicked my skin. Leaning forward, he lapped the blood pooling on the surface.

My knees buckled. Fire scorched my veins, soaring through my body so hard and fast it stole my breath. Wyatt wrapped his arms around me, holding me tight as he drew a long, gentle pull into his mouth. Tiny pinpricks of light exploded before my eyes, surrounding the two of us in a magical cocoon of sparkles. Stars. The same stars he'd created in the cave now burst from the ceiling in my bedroom.

When he eased back, a hunger flamed in his eyes. "Do you see it?"

"The lights?"

He swept his fingers over my cheek. "Our lights."

"It's..." I couldn't find the words.

Deep orange, yellow, and pink bursts exploded above us. The colors of sunrise.

Of new beginnings.

Overwhelmed with emotion, I crushed my lips against his. The taste of my blood swirled with his inside my mouth, heightening the tingles colliding between my legs. So many emotions swept through me. Love and affection. Dedication. Admiration. With this kiss, I gave him my whole heart.

Breathing heavy, Wyatt eased back and captured my face in his strong hands, peering through my eyes, right to the heart of my soul. "It's our union. Our forever."

Looking for your next book boyfriend? Fall for Cassie's award-winning steamy bad boy angel series, **The Fallen Guardians**! These heroes bring down Hell for the woman they love. Start the series today with Unforsaken.

ACKNOWLEDGEMENTS

As the Small Town Packs series comes to an end, I'm sad but also incredibly humbled by all the love for these stories. I've always had a soft spot for small-town romance so pairing it with shifters was a no-brainer for me! But I could never have expected the amount of reader support for these characters. It totally blew me away. So, thank you! Thank you for your reviews, your kind words, your shares, and your encouragement to write a series so close to my heart. Without readers like you, I couldn't open my laptop every day and do what I love.

These characters have definitely sparked ideas for future books, and although this series has ended, I don't think it'll be the last time you hear from them.

Until next time,

Cassie x

P/S If you love bonus content, including flash fiction and character interviews, join my monthly newsletter to access all the freebies!!

ALSO BY CASSIE LAELYN

The Fallen Guardians

Unforsaken (Book 1)

Unforgotten (Book 2)

Unseen (Book 3)

Untamed (Book 4)

Small Town Packs

Salvation (Wolves of Woodland Falls)

Reclaim (Cedar Valley Bears)

Awaken (Wolves of Timber Falls)

ABOUT THE AUTHOR

Cassie is an award-winning paranormal romance author living in sunny Queensland, Australia with her husband and two BMX-crazy boys.

She has a passion for crafting stories involving loyal, otherworldly characters in need of love and redemption. She's also a self-confessed chocoholic and a huge sucker for an angsty, gut-wrenching happily ever after.

When she isn't narrating imaginary characters, Cassie loves binging on TV shows, spending time at the beach, and curling up listening to the rain.

Join Cassie's newsletter (www.cassielaelyn.com) to stay up to date with release information, giveaways and access the subscriber's only area for free reads to devour between book releases.